William Shakespeare

The Comedy of As You Like It

William Shakespeare

The Comedy of As You Like It

ISBN/EAN: 9783744788489

Printed in Europe, USA, Canada, Australia, Japan

Cover: Foto ©Andreas Hilbeck / pixelio.de

More available books at **www.hansebooks.com**

THE COMEDY

OF

AS YOU LIKE IT

BY

WILLIAM SHAKESPEARE

NEW YORK · : · CINCINNATI · : · CHICAGO

AMERICAN BOOK COMPANY

1895

Printed by
William Ivison
New York, U. S. A.

INTRODUCTION.

"As You Like It" was on the stage as early as the year 1600, but was not in print till it appeared in the first collection of Shakespeare's plays, published in 1623 and known as the "First Folio."

The comedy is founded on a novel by Thomas Lodge, printed in 1590 under the title of "Rosalynde, Euphues' Golden Legacie."

Shakespeare borrows names and incidents from this story, but the characterization is his own; and his creative genius has surrounded "a rather heavy and commonplace tale with an atmosphere of graceful romance, resulting in a play the charming animation and grace of which have made it the delight of all readers, young and old."

The action of "As You Like It" is wholly in the open air, and the drama is redolent of woods and green fields and all the charms of a pastoral and rustic life. After the first act its incidents are for the most part in the Forest of Arden, where a Duke, dispossessed of his title and dukedom by Frederick, a usurping younger brother, is living in banishment in the company of many friends and adherents. Here, in genial comradeship, enlivened by the songs of the tuneful Amiens, and entertained with the sententious philosophizing of "the melancholy Jaques,"—a traveled courtier, highly appreciated by the Duke,—they "fleet the time carelessly" as in the golden age, and, "exempt from public haunt," find

> "Tongues in trees, books in the running brooks,
> Sermons in stones, and good in everything."

The play opens, however, in a garden near the house of Oliver, the eldest son of Sir Rowland de Bois, where we learn from a conversation between Orlando and Adam—an old servant of the family—that Sir Rowland, at his death, bequeathed his possessions to his three sons, of whom Orlando is the youngest, leaving the management and distribution of the estate to Oliver. The latter is also charged with the training of Orlando, but entertains a groundless and unnatural hatred for him, treating him with the utmost indignity, withholding his inheritance, and denying him the education fitting his birth.

While Orlando and Adam are talking, Oliver enters, and a violent quarrel ensues between the brothers. Exasperated by the contemptuous taunts of Oliver, Orlando seizes him by the throat, and they are only separated through the intervention of Adam. When he and Orlando go out, Charles, a noted wrestler, one of Duke Frederick's retainers, comes in to advise Oliver to prevent Orlando's intention to enter the lists in a contest arranged for the following day, as it would go hard with the young man should he do so, since he (Charles) contends for his reputation at this meeting. But Oliver discloses to Charles the feeling he has towards his brother, gives him a bad character, and says he would as soon see Orlando's neck broken as his finger.

The next scene is a lawn before Duke Frederick's palace, where Celia, his daughter, and Rosalind, daughter of his exiled brother, are seated. Le Beau, a courtier, appears, and tells them they will see some rare sport if they remain, as it is on this lawn that the wrestlers are to meet for the final struggle of the tournament. They decide to stay. Charles and Orlando approach. The ladies, admiring the youth and comeliness of Orlando, endeavor to dissuade him from an undertaking in which his youth and inexperience would be no match for the strength and skill of his opponent. But Orlando, though flattered by the interest they show for him, will not withdraw his challenge, and to the surprise of all overthrows the champion, who is borne senseless from the scene. Frederick, being informed that Orlando is a son of Sir Rowland de Bois, whom he declares to have ever been his enemy, turns coldly from the victor, offering neither praise nor reward. Not so Rosalind, who, already favorably impressed with the handsome and courageous youth, quite loses her heart to the modest athlete when she learns that he is the son of a steadfast friend of her father. As for Orlando, he had fallen desperately in love with Rosalind at first sight.

Now Duke Frederick, who, out of regard for the sisterly affection and lifelong intimacy existing between Celia and her cousin, had retained Rosalind at his court when he expelled her father, suddenly warns her, on the pretense of her being a traitor, to leave his palace and dominions within ten days, or forfeit her life. Celia, hearing this, assures her cousin that in banishing her the Duke has banished his daughter as well, as she will share Rosalind's exile and follow her fortunes.

And the two—Rosalind masquerading as a young forester, and Celia in the costume of a shepherdess—accompanied by

Touchstone, a "clownish fool" of the Duke's household, steal from the court, and wend their way to the Forest of Arden, where Rosalind goes to seek her father. Frederick, alarmed by his daughter's absence, and having reason to suspect that Orlando, who is also missing, may be with the runaways, sends for Oliver, commands him to find his brother, and sequesters his lands and goods till he does so.

In the mean time Orlando, having information from the faithful Adam that his life is in danger from the increased bitterness of Oliver's enmity, has abandoned his brother's house, and, wandering aimlessly, comes upon the exiled Duke in the woods of Arden, and is hospitably welcomed. But adversity has by no means abated the ardor of Orlando's love for Rosalind, and to relieve his passion he writes verses in her praise, which he fastens to the trees of the forest. These Celia and Rosalind discover, and are thus made aware of Orlando's presence in their neighborhood. They soon meet him. Orlando, of course, does not recognize either of the cousins in their disguise; but finding the young forester — as he takes Rosalind to be — a sprightly youth of more refined manners than one would look to meet in "so removed a dwelling," he becomes confidential, and imparts to her something of his history and his love. Rosalind ridicules his lovesickness; tells him "love is merely a madness, and . . . deserves as well a dark house and a whip as madmen do;" that, profiting by the experience and instruction of an old religious uncle, she professes to cure such madness; that Orlando does not look like a lover — has none of her uncle's marks upon him; but she says "there is a man haunts the forest, that abuses our young plants with carving 'Rosalind' on their barks; hangs odes upon hawthorns and elegies on brambles, all, forsooth, deifying the name of Rosalind. If I could meet that fancymonger, I would give him some good counsel, for he seems to have the quotidian of love upon him." Orlando assures her he is the man "that is so love-shaked," but does not care to be cured, doubts her ability to cure him, and asks if she has ever cured any one. "Yes, one," she answers, "and in this manner. He was to imagine me his love, his mistress; and I set him every day to woo me; at which time would I, being but a moonish youth, grieve, be effeminate, changeable, longing and liking, proud, fantastical, apish, shallow, inconstant, full of tears, full of smiles; . . . would now like him, now loathe him; . . . now weep for him, then spit at him," till at length "I drave my suitor from his mad humor of love. . . . And thus I cur'd him; and this way . . . I would cure you, if you would but call me Rosalind and come every day to my cote and woo me." Orlando insists that he has no desire to be cured, but is induced to go with Celia and Rosalind to their cottage to try the efficacy of the remedy.

One day, while undergoing this treatment, Orlando, quitting Rosalind for an hour to keep an appointment with the Duke, whom he serves, chances upon a man sleeping under an oak, around whose neck a serpent is coiling itself, while near by a lioness crouches, awaiting some movement of the sleeper to spring upon him. At Orlando's approach the serpent glides away, and he discovers the imperiled man to be Oliver, the cruel brother from whose malignity he has suffered so much and so unjustly. The first impulse is to leave him to his fate;

> "But kindness, nobler ever than revenge,
>   And nature, stronger than his just occasion,"

prevail, and he attacks and kills the lioness.

Oliver, awakening, recognizes his brother; forgiveness and reconciliation follow, and he is sent by Orlando to apologize to Rosalind for his failure to return as promised, and to exhibit a napkin which Orlando had used to stanch a wound received in his encounter with the beast. At the sight of blood Rosalind swoons, but, reviving, would have Oliver believe the fainting counterfeited, that he might report to Orlando how well she had feigned. But her agitation increasing, Oliver, at Celia's request, assists in leading Rosalind to their cottage, and on the way becomes interested in Celia, wins her love, and, returning to Orlando, says if he will consent to their marriage, he (Oliver) will surrender to his brother all the revenue that was old Sir Rowland's, and live and die a shepherd in the forest.

There is a lively episode in the play, of Phebe, a beautiful shepherdess, and Silvius, her lover, whose earnest pleadings she treats with cruel scorn. Rosalind, rambling through the wood, happens to meet with them. She rates the girl roundly for her proud and disdainful bearing, saying that though she may have some beauty she is not for all markets, and that she would do well to take her lover's offer, "and thank Heaven, fasting, for a good man's love." At the same time she tells Silvius that he is a fool for following the shepherdess, for he is "a thousand times a properer man than she a woman;" whereupon Phebe straightway falls in love with Rosalind (in her male attire), and begs her to "chide a year together;" for she would rather hear her chide than Silvius woo.

Rosalind, having now satisfied herself of the truth and constancy of Orlando's love for her, informs him that she can do strange things, and if he so desires she will produce his real and very Rosalind, whom, with the Duke's permission, he may marry at the wedding of Oliver and Celia, which is to take place at the Duke's cave the next day. She also promises Phebe that she will then marry her if she (Rosalind) ever marries woman, Phebe readily agreeing to take Silvius for her husband in case she rejects Rosalind. Accordingly, when all meet at the Duke's, Rosalind, appearing in her own character, gives her hand to the astonished and delighted Orlando, Celia weds Oliver, Phebe keeps her word and accepts Silvius, and Touchstone, coming in with Audrey, an unsophisticated lass of the forest, of whom he has become enamored, adds another couple

> " To join in Hymen's bands."

In the midst of these festivities the second son of Sir Rowland de Bois arrives to announce that Frederick, the usurping Duke, having set out with an armed force to take his brother and put him to the sword, was met on the skirts of the wood by an old religious man, and by him converted

> " Both from his enterprise and from the world;
> His crown bequeathing to his banish'd brother,
> And all their lands restor'd to them again
> That were with him exil'd."

And so, amid general rejoicing, the play concludes with a merry dance by the characters.

Of "As You Like It," Professor Dowden ("Shakespeare: His Plays and Poems") says: "The story is taken from Thomas Lodge's prose tale, 'Rosalynde, Euphues' Golden Legacie;' and a passage in Lodge's dedication probably suggested to Shakespeare the name of his play. In parts of his work the dramatist follows the story-teller closely, but there are some important differences. The heroic names, Orlando, Oliver, and Sir Rowland, are due to Shakespeare. It was a thought of Shakespeare to make the rightful and the usurping Dukes brothers. . . . To Shakespeare we owe the creation of the characters of Jaques, Touchstone, and Audrey. . . . 'Sweet are the uses of adversity,' moralizes the banished Duke, and external, material adversity has come to him, to Rosalind, and to Orlando; but if fortune is harsh, nature—both external nature and human character—is sound and sweet, and of real suffering there is none in the play. All that is evil remains in the society which the denizens of the forest have left behind; and both seriously —in the characters of the usurping Duke and Oliver—and playfully—through Touchstone's mockery of court follies—a criticism on what is evil and artificial in society is suggested in contrast with the woodland life; yet Shakespeare never falls into the conventional pastoral manner. Orlando is an ideal of youthful strength, beauty, and noble innocence of heart; and Rosalind's bright, tender womanhood seems but to grow more exquisitely feminine in the male attire which she has assumed in self-defense. . . . Possessed of a delightful consciousness of power to confer happiness, she can dally with disguises, and make what is most serious to her at the same time possess the charm of an exquisite frolic."

Hazlitt ("Characters of Shakespeare's Plays") remarks of "As You Like It:" "It is the most ideal of any of Shakespeare's plays. It is a pastoral drama, in which the interest arises more out of the sentiments and characters than out of the actions or situations. It is not what is done, but what is said, that claims our attention. Nursed in solitude 'under the shade of melancholy boughs,' the imagination grows soft and delicate, and the wit runs riot in idleness, like a spoiled child that is never sent to school. Caprice and fancy reign and revel here, and stern necessity is banished to the court. . . . The very air of the place seems to breathe a spirit of philosophical poetry. . . . Never was there such beautiful moralizing, equally free from pedantry or petulance. Jaques is the only purely contemplative character in Shakespeare. . . . His whole occupation is to amuse his mind, and he is totally regardless of his body and his fortunes. He is the prince of philosophical idlers; . . . he sets no value upon anything but as it serves as food for reflection. He can 'suck melancholy out of a song, as a weasel sucks eggs;' the motley fool, who 'morals on the time,' is the greatest prize he meets with in the forest. He resents Orlando's love for Rosalind as some disparagement of his own passion for abstract truth; and leaves the Duke as soon as he is restored to his sovereignty, to seek his brother out, who has quitted it and turned hermit. . . . Touchstone is a rare fellow. He is a mixture of the ancient cynic philosopher with the modern buffoon, and turns folly into wit and wit into folly, just as the fit takes him. . . . There is hardly any one of Shakespeare's plays that contains a greater number of passages that have been quoted in books of extracts, or a greater number of phrases that have become in a measure proverbial. If we were to give all the striking passages we should give half the play. We will only recall a few of the most delightful to the reader's recollection. Such are the meeting between Orlando and Adam;[1] the exquisite appeal of Orlando to the humanity of the Duke and his company to supply him with food for the old man, and their answer;[2] the Duke's description of a country life, and the

---

[1] Act ii., sc. 3, p. 37.   [2] Act ii., sc. 7, p. 49.

account of Jaques's moralizing on the wounded deer;[1] his meeting with Touchstone in the forest;[2] his apology for his own melancholy and his satirical vein, and the well-known speech on the stages of human life;[3] the old song of 'Blow, blow, thou winter wind;'[4] Rosalind's description of the marks of a lover, and of the progress of time with different persons;[5] . . . Touchstone's lecture to the shepherd;[6] . . . his panegyric on the virtues of 'an If;'[7] . . . and Phebe's description of Ganymede at the end of the third act."[8]

Mrs. Jameson, in her "Characteristics of Women," thus delineates the women of this comedy: "Though Rosalind is a princess, she is a princess of Arcady; and notwithstanding the charming effect produced by her first scenes, we scarcely ever think of her with a reference to them, or associate her with a court and the artificial appendages of her rank. She was not made to 'lord it o'er a fair mansion,' and take state upon her, like the all-accomplished Portia; but to breathe the free air of heaven and frolic among green leaves. . . . She was not made to bandy wit with lords, and tread courtly measures with plumed and warlike cavaliers, . . . but to dance on the greensward, and 'murmur among living brooks a music sweeter than their own.' . . . Everything about Rosalind breathes of 'youth and youth's sweet prime.' She is fresh as the morning, sweet as the dew-awakened blossoms, and light as the breeze that plays among them. . . . Her volubility is like the bird's song; it is the outpouring of a heart filled to overflowing with life, love, and joy, and all sweet and

---

[1] Act ii., sc. 1, p. 35.   [2] Act ii., sc. 7, p. 46.
[3] Act ii., sc. 7, p. 50.   [4] Act ii., sc. 7, p. 52.
[5] Act iii., sc. 2, p. 63.   [6] Act v., sc. 1, p. 89.
[7] Act v., sc. 4, p. 98.   [8] Page 74.

affectionate impulses. . . . As her vivacity never lessens our impression of her sensibility, so she wears her masculine attire without the slightest impugnment of her delicacy. Shakespeare did not make the modesty of his women depend on their dress. . . . Rosalind has in truth 'no doublet and hose in her disposition.' How her heart seems to throb and flutter under her page's vest ! What depth of love in her passion for Orlando, whether disguised beneath a saucy playfulness, or breaking forth with a fond impatience, or half betrayed in that beautiful scene where she faints at the sight of the kerchief stained with his blood ! . . . Then how beautifully is the dialogue managed between herself and Orlando ! How well she assumes the airs of a saucy page without throwing off her feminine sweetness ! How her wit flutters free as air over every subject ! With what a careless grace, yet with what exquisite propriety ! . . . Rosalind has not the impressive eloquence of Portia. . . . Her longest speeches are not her best; nor is her taunting address to Phebe, beautiful and celebrated as it is, equal to Phebe's own description of her. The latter, indeed, is more in earnest.

"Celia is more quiet and retired; but she rather yields to Rosalind than is eclipsed by her. She is as full of sweetness, kindness, and intelligence, quite as susceptible, and almost as witty, though she makes less display of wit. She is described as less fair and less gifted; yet the attempt to excite in her mind a jealousy of her lovelier friend, by placing them in comparison, fails to awaken in the generous heart of Celia any other feeling than an increased tenderness and sympathy for her cousin. To Celia Shakespeare has given some of the most striking and animated parts of the dialogue; and in particular that exquisite description of the friendship between her and Rosalind :

> ' We still have slept together,
> Rose at an instant, learn'd, play'd, eat together,
> And wheresoe'er we went, like Juno's swans,
> Still we went coupled and inseparable.'

"Phebe is quite an Arcadian coquette; she is a piece of pastoral poetry. Audrey is only rustic. A very amusing effect is produced by the contrast between the frank and free bearing of the two princesses in disguise and the scornful airs of the real shepherdess. In the speeches of Phebe, and in the dialogue between her and Silvius, Shakespeare has anticipated all the beauties of the Italian pastoral, and surpassed Tasso and Guarini. We find two among the most poetical passages of the play appropriated to Phebe,—the taunting speech to Silvius, and the description of Rosalind in her page's costume."

A peculiar interest attaches to the subordinate but fine character of Adam, arising from a tradition, current in the last century, that Shakespeare had himself personated the part on the stage. The story is neither more nor less authentic than much of the little that has come down to us of Shakespeare's personal history.

AS YOU LIKE IT.

PERSONS OF THE PLAY.

DUKE, *living in banishment.*
FREDERICK, *his brother, and usurper of his dominions.*
AMIENS, } *lords attending on the ban-*
JAQUES, } *ished Duke.*
LE BEAU, *a courtier attending upon Frederick.*
CHARLES, *wrestler to Frederick.*
OLIVER, }
JAQUES, } *sons of Sir Rowland de*
ORLANDO, } *Bois.*
ADAM, } *servants to Oliver.*
DENNIS, }
TOUCHSTONE, *a clown.*

SIR OLIVER MARTEXT, *a vicar.*
CORIN, } *shepherds.*
SILVIUS, }
WILLIAM, *a country fellow, in love with Audrey.*
A person representing Hymen.

ROSALIND, *daughter to the banished Duke.*
CELIA, *daughter to Frederick.*
PHEBE, *a shepherdess.*
AUDREY, *a country wench.*

Lords, pages and attendants, etc.

SCENE: *Oliver's house; Duke Frederick's court; and the Forest of Arden.*

ACT I.

SCENE I. *Orchard of Oliver's House.*

Enter ORLANDO *and* ADAM.

Orlando. As I remember, Adam, it was upon this fashion: he bequeathed me by will but poor a¹ thousand crowns, and, as thou say'st, charg'd my brother, on his blessing, to breed me well; and there begins my sadness. My brother Jaques he keeps at school, and report speaks goldenly of his profit;² for my part,

---

¹ This transposition of the indefinite article occurs elsewhere in Shakespeare.
² Proficiency.

he keeps me rustically at home, or, to speak more properly, stays me here at home unkept; for call you that keeping for a gentleman of my birth, that differs not from the stalling of an ox? His horses are bred better; for, besides that they are fair with their feeding, they are taught their manage,[1] and to that end riders dearly hir'd; but I, his brother, gain nothing under him but growth, for the which his animals on his dunghills are as much bound to him as I. Besides this nothing that he so plentifully gives me, the something that nature gave me his countenance[2] seems to take from me: he lets me feed with his hinds,[3] bars me the place of a brother, and, as much as in him lies, mines[4] my gentility with my education. This is it, Adam, that grieves me; and the spirit of my father, which I think is within me, begins to mutiny against this servitude. I will no longer endure it, though yet I know no wise remedy how to avoid it.

Adam. Yonder comes my master, your brother.

Orlando. Go apart, Adam, and thou shalt hear how he will shake me up.

Enter OLIVER.

Oliver. Now, sir! what make you here?[5]

Orlando. Nothing; I am not taught to make anything.

Oliver. What mar you then, sir?

Orlando. Marry,[6] sir, I am helping you to mar that which God made — a poor unworthy brother of yours — with idleness.

Oliver. Marry, sir, be better employed, and be naught awhile.[7]

Orlando. Shall I keep your hogs and eat husks with them? What prodigal portion[8] have I spent, that I should come to such penury?

---

[1] The training of a horse.　　　[2] Treatment.　　　[3] Farm laborers.

[4] Undermines.

[5] "What make," etc., i.e., what are you doing here?

[6] A petty oath from the name of the Virgin Mary.

[7] "Be naught awhile," used as a malediction; as, "Efface yourself!" "Plague on you!" or the like.

[8] See Luke xv. 11-32.

Oliver. Know you where you are, sir?

Orlando. O sir, very well: here in your orchard.

Oliver. Know you before whom, sir?

Orlando. Ay, better than him I am before knows me. I know you are my eldest brother; and, in the gentle condition of blood, you should so know me. The courtesy of nations allows you my better, in that you are the firstborn; but the same tradition takes not away my blood, were there twenty brothers betwixt us. I have as much of my father in me as you; albeit, I confess, your coming before me is nearer to his reverence.

Oliver. What, boy!

Orlando. Come, come, elder brother, you are too young in this.

Oliver. Wilt thou lay hands on me, villain?

Orlando. I am no villain; I am the youngest son of Sir Rowland de Bois; he was my father, and he is thrice a villain that says such a father begot villains. Wert thou not my brother, I would not take this hand from thy throat till this other had pull'd out thy tongue for saying so. Thou hast rail'd on thyself.

Adam. Sweet masters, be patient; for your father's remembrance, be at accord.

Oliver. Let me go, I say.

Orlando. I will not, till I please; you shall hear me. My father charg'd you in his will to give me good education; you have train'd me like a peasant, obscuring and hiding from me all gentlemanlike qualities. The spirit of my father grows strong in me, and I will no longer endure it; therefore allow me such exercises as may become a gentleman, or give me the poor allottery [1] my father left me by testament; with that I will go buy my fortunes.

Oliver. And what wilt thou do—beg?—when that is spent? Well, sir, get you in; I will not long be troubled with you; you shall have some part of your will. I pray you, leave me.

Orlando. I will no further offend you than becomes me for my good.

---

[1] Portion.

2

Oliver. Get you with him, you old dog!

Adam. Is "old dog" my reward? Most true, I have lost my teeth in your service. God be with my old master! He would not have spoke[1] such a word.   [*Exeunt Orlando and Adam.*

Oliver. Is it even so? begin you to grow[2] upon me? I will physic your rankness, and yet give no thousand crowns neither.— Holla, Dennis!

Enter DENNIS.

Dennis. Calls your worship?

Oliver. Was not Charles, the Duke's wrestler, here to speak with me?

Dennis. So please you, he is here at the door and importunes access to you.

Oliver. Call him in. [*Exit Dennis.*] 'Twill be a good way; and to-morrow the wrestling is.

Enter CHARLES.

Charles. Good morrow to your worship.

Oliver. Good Monsieur Charles, what's the new news at the new court?

Charles. There's no news at the court, sir, but the old news: that is, the old Duke is banish'd by his younger brother the new Duke; and three or four loving lords have put themselves into voluntary exile with him, whose lands and revenues enrich the new Duke; therefore he gives them good leave to wander.

Oliver. Can you tell if Rosalind, the Duke's daughter, be banish'd with her father?

Charles. O no; for the Duke's daughter, her cousin, so loves her—being ever from their cradles bred together—that she would have follow'd her exile, or have died to stay behind her. She is at the court, and no less beloved of her uncle than his own daughter; and never two ladies loved as they do.

Oliver. Where will the old Duke live?

<hr>

[1] Spoken.   [2] Encroach.

Charles. They say he is already in the Forest of Arden, and a many merry men with him; and there they live like the old Robin Hood [1] of England. They say many young gentlemen flock to him every day, and fleet the time carelessly,[2] as they did in the golden world.[3]

Oliver. What, you wrestle to-morrow before the new Duke?

Charles. Marry, do I, sir; and I came to acquaint you with a matter. I am given, sir, secretly to understand that your younger brother Orlando hath a disposition to come in disguis'd against me to try a fall. To-morrow, sir, I wrestle for my credit; and he that escapes me without some broken limb shall acquit him well. Your brother is but young and tender; and, for your love, I would be loath to foil him, as I must, for my own honor, if he come in. Therefore, out of my love to you, I came hither to acquaint you withal, that either you might stay him from his intendment, or brook such disgrace well as he shall run into, in that it is a thing of his own search and altogether against my will.

Oliver. Charles, I thank thee for thy love to me, which thou shalt find I will most kindly requite. I had myself notice of my brother's purpose herein, and have by underhand means labored to dissuade him from it; but he is resolute. I'll tell thee, Charles: it is the stubbornest young fellow of France; full of ambition, an envious emulator of every man's good parts, a secret and villainous contriver against me, his natural brother. Therefore use thy discretion; I had as lief thou didst break his neck as his finger. And thou wert best look to't; for if thou dost him any slight

---

1 Robin Hood, "the English balladsinger's joy," was the ideal yeoman of the people of England, as Arthur was the ideal knight of the upper classes. He figures in the ballads as an outlaw, "robbing the rich to endow the poor; a great sportsman; the incomparable archer; the lover of the greenwood and of a free life; brave, adventurous, jovial, open-handed, and a protector of women."

2 "Fleet the time carelessly," i.e., void of care, cause the time to pass swiftly.

3 "The golden world," i.e., the golden age fabled by the ancient poets.

disgrace, or if he do not mightily grace himself on thee, he will practice [1] against thee by poison, entrap thee by some treacherous device, and never leave thee till he hath ta'en thy life by some indirect means or other; for, I assure thee—and almost with tears I speak it—there is not one so young and so villainous this day living. I speak but brotherly of him; but should I anatomize [2] him to thee as he is, I must blush and weep, and thou must look pale and wonder.

Charles. I am heartily glad I came hither to you. If he come to-morrow, I'll give him his payment. If ever he go alone again, I'll never wrestle for prize more; and so God keep your worship!

Oliver. Farewell, good Charles. [*Exit Charles.*] Now will I stir this gamester. [3] I hope I shall see an end of him; for my soul—yet I know not why—hates nothing more than he. Yet he's gentle, never school'd and yet learned, full of noble device, [4] of all sorts enchantingly beloved, and indeed so much in the heart of the world, and especially of my own people, who best know him, that I am altogether misprized. [5] But it shall not be so long; this wrestler shall clear all. Nothing remains but that I kindle the boy thither, [6] which now I'll go about. [*Exit.*

Scene II. *Lawn before the Duke's Palace.*

Enter CELIA *and* ROSALIND.

Celia. I pray thee, Rosalind, sweet my coz, be merry.

Rosalind. Dear Celia, I show more mirth than I am mistress of; and would you yet I were merrier? Unless you could teach me to forget a banished father, you must not learn [7] me how to remember any extraordinary pleasure.

1 Plot.   2 Expose.   3 Sporting youth.
4 Aims.   5 Undervalued.
6 "Kindle," etc., i.e., excite him to take part in this contest.
7 Teach.

Celia. Herein I see thou lov'st me not with the full weight that I love thee. If my uncle, thy banished father, had banished thy uncle, the Duke, my father, so thou hadst been still with me I could have taught my love to take thy father for mine. So wouldst thou if the truth of thy love to me were so righteously temper'd [1] as mine is to thee.

Rosalind. Well, I will forget the condition of my estate, to rejoice in yours.

Celia. You know my father hath no child but I,[2] nor none is like to have; and, truly, when he dies, thou shalt be his heir; for what he hath taken away from thy father perforce, I will render thee again in affection; by mine honor, I will; and when I break that oath, let me turn monster. Therefore, my sweet Rose, my dear Rose, be merry.

Rosalind. From henceforth I will, coz, and devise sports. Let me see: what think you of falling in love?

Celia. Marry, I prithee, do, to make sport withal; but love no man in good earnest; nor no further in sport, neither, than with safety of a pure blush thou mayst in honor come off again.

Rosalind. What shall be our sport then?

Celia. Let us sit and mock the good housewife Fortune[3] from her wheel, that her gifts may henceforth be bestowed equally.

Rosalind. I would we could do so, for her benefits are mightily misplaced, and the bountiful blind woman doth most mistake in her gifts to women.

Celia. 'Tis true; for those that she makes fair she scarce makes honest, and those that she makes honest she makes very ill-favoredly.

Rosalind. Nay, now thou goest from Fortune's office to Nature's. Fortune reigns in gifts of the world, not in the lineaments of Nature.

---

[1] Composed.   [2] Me.

[3] The goddess of fortune of classical mythology is represented with a horn of plenty at her side. She is blindfolded, and generally holds a wheel, a symbol of inconstancy, in her hand.

Enter TOUCHSTONE.

Celia. No ? when Nature hath made a fair creature, may she
not by Fortune fall into the fire ?   Though Nature hath given
us wit to flout at Fortune, hath not Fortune sent in this fool to
cut off the argument ?

Rosalind. Indeed, there is Fortune too hard for Nature, when
Fortune makes Nature's natural[1] the cutter-off of Nature's wit.

Celia. Peradventure this is not Fortune's work neither, but
Nature's, who, perceiving our natural wits too dull to reason of
such goddesses, hath sent this natural for our whetstone; for
always the dullness of the fool is the whetstone of the wits. —
How now, wit ! whither wander you ?

Touchstone. Mistress, you must come away to your father.

Celia. Were you made the messenger ?

Touchstone. No, by mine honor, but I was bid to come for
you.

Rosalind. Where learned you that oath, fool ?

Touchstone. Of a certain knight that swore by his honor they
were good pancakes, and swore by his honor the mustard was
naught.[2]   Now I'll stand to it, the pancakes were naught and
the mustard was good, and yet was not the knight forsworn.

Celia. How prove you that, in the great heap of your knowledge ?

Rosalind. Ay, marry, now unmuzzle your wisdom.

Touchstone. Stand you both forth now.   Stroke your chins,
and swear by your beards that I am a knave.

Celia. By our beards, if we had them, thou art.

Touchstone. By my knavery, if I had it, then I were : but if
you swear by that that is not, you are not forsworn.   No more
was this knight, swearing by his honor, for he never had any ;
or, if he had, he had sworn it away before ever he saw those
pancakes or that mustard.

Celia. Prithee, who is't that thou mean'st ?

---

[1] Fool.   [2] Bad.

Touchstone. One that old Frederick, your father, loves.

Celia. My father's love is enough to honor him.   Enough ! speak no more of him ; you'll be whipp'd for taxation[1] one of these days.

Touchstone. The more pity that fools may not speak wisely what wise men do foolishly.

Celia. By my troth, thou sayest true ; for since the little wit that fools have was silenced, the little foolery that wise men have makes a great show.   Here comes Monsieur Le Beau.

Rosalind. With his mouth full of news.

Celia. Which he will put on us, as pigeons feed their young.

Rosalind. Then shall we be news-cramm'd.

Celia. All the better ; we shall be the more marketable.—

Enter LE BEAU.

Bon jour, Monsieur Le Beau ; what's the news ?

Le Beau. Fair princess, you have lost much good sport.

Celia. Sport ! of what color ?

Le Beau. What color, madam ! how shall I answer you ?

Rosalind. As wit and fortune will.

Touchstone. Or as the Destinies decree.

Celia. Well said.   That was laid on with a trowel.

Touchstone. Nay, if I keep not my rank,—

Rosalind. Thou losest thy old smell.

Le Beau. You amaze[3] me, ladies.   I would have told you of good wrestling, which you have lost the sight of.

Rosalind. Yet tell us the manner of the wrestling.

Le Beau. I will tell you the beginning ; and, if it please your ladyships, you may see the end, for the best is yet to do ; and here, where you are, they are coming to perform it.

Celia. Well,—the beginning, that is dead and buried.

Le Beau. There comes an old man and his three sons,—

Celia. I could match this beginning with an old tale.

---

[1] Slander.   [2] Kind.   [3] Bewilder.

Le Beau. Three proper [1] young men, of excellent growth and presence.

Rosalind. With bills on their necks, " Be it known unto all men by these presents."

Le Beau. The eldest of the three wrestled with Charles, the Duke's wrestler; which Charles in a moment threw him and broke three of his ribs, that there is little hope of life in him. So he serv'd the second, and so the third. Yonder they lie; the poor old man, their father, making such pitiful dole [2] over them that all the beholders take his part with weeping.

Rosalind. Alas !

Touchstone. But what is the sport, monsieur, that the ladies have lost ?

Le Beau. Why, this that I speak of.

Touchstone. Thus men may grow wiser every day ! It is the first time that ever I heard breaking of ribs was sport for ladies.

Celia. Or I, I promise thee.

Rosalind. But is there any else longs to see this broken music in his sides ? is there yet another dotes upon rib-breaking ? — Shall we see this wrestling, cousin ?

Le Beau. You must, if you stay here; for here is the place appointed for the wrestling, and they are ready to perform it.

Celia. Yonder, sure, they are coming; let us now stay and see it.

Flourish. Enter DUKE FREDERICK, Lords, ORLANDO, CHARLES, *and* Attendants.

Duke F. Come on; since the youth will not be entreated, his own peril on his forwardness.

Rosalind. Is yonder the man ?

Le Beau. Even he, madam.

---

[1] Fine-looking.   [2] Lamentation.

Celia. Alas, he is too young! yet he looks successfully.[1]

Duke F. How now, daughter and cousin![2] are you crept hither to see the wrestling?

Rosalind. Ay, my liege, so please you give us leave.

Duke F. You will take little delight in it, I can tell you; there is such odds in the men. In pity of the challenger's youth I would fain dissuade him, but he will not be entreated. Speak to him, ladies; see if you can move him.

Celia. Call him hither, good Monsieur Le Beau.

Duke F. Do so; I'll not be by. [*Duke goes apart.*

Le Beau. Monsieur the challenger, the princess calls for you.

Orlando. I attend them with all respect and duty.

Rosalind. Young man, have you challeng'd Charles the wrestler?

Orlando. No, fair princess; he is the general challenger. I come but in, as others do, to try with him the strength of my youth.

Celia. Young gentleman, your spirits are too bold for your years. You have seen cruel proof of this man's strength. If you saw yourself with your eyes or knew yourself with your judgment, the fear of your adventure would counsel you to a more equal enterprise. We pray you, for your own sake, to embrace your own safety and give over this attempt.

Rosalind. Do, young sir; your reputation shall not therefore be misprized. We will make it our suit to the Duke that the wrestling might not go forward.

Orlando. I beseech you, punish me not with your hard thoughts, wherein I confess me much guilty, to deny so fair and excellent ladies anything. But let your fair eyes and gentle wishes go with me to my trial, wherein if I be foil'd, there is but one sham'd that was never gracious;[3] if kill'd, but one dead that is willing to be so. I shall do my friends no wrong, for I have

---

1 As if he would win.

2 "Cousin," in Shakespeare's time, was used indifferently for all degrees of kindred beyond the first.   3 Favored.

none to lament me; the world no injury, for in it I have nothing; only in the world I fill up a place which may be better supplied when I have made it empty.

Rosalind. The little strength that I have, I would it were with you.

Celia. And mine, to eke out hers.

Rosalind. Fare you well. Pray Heaven I be deceiv'd in you !

Celia. Your heart's desires be with you !

Charles. Come, where is this young gallant that is so desirous to lie with his mother earth ?

Orlando. Ready, sir; but his will hath in it a more modest working.

Duke F. You shall try but one fall.

Charles. No, I warrant your grace, you shall not entreat him to a second, that have so mightily persuaded him from a first.

Orlando. You mean to mock me after; you should not have mock'd me before. But come your ways.

Rosalind. Now Hercules[1] be thy speed,[2] young man !

Celia. I would I were invisible, to catch the strong fellow by the leg.   [*They wrestle.*

Rosalind. O excellent young man !

Celia. If I had a thunderbolt in mine eye, I can tell who should down.   [*Shout. Charles is thrown.*

Duke F. No more, no more.

Orlando. Yes, I beseech your grace. I am not yet well breath'd.

Duke F. How dost thou, Charles ?

Le Beau. He cannot speak, my lord.

Duke F. Bear him away.—What is thy name, young man ?

Orlando. Orlando, my liege; the youngest son of Sir Rowland de Bois.

Duke F. I would thou hadst been son to some man else !
The world esteem'd thy father honorable,

---

[1] A mythological hero of antiquity, celebrated for his feats of strength.
[2] " Be thy speed," i.e., speed you; help you.

But I did find him still mine enemy.
Thou shouldst have better pleas'd me with this deed
Hadst thou descended from another house.
But fare thee well; thou art a gallant youth.
I would thou hadst told me of another father.

      [*Exeunt Duke Frederick, train, and Le Beau.*

 Celia. Were I my father, coz, would I do this?

 Orlando. I am more proud to be Sir Rowland's son,—
His youngest son,—and would not change that calling
To be adopted heir to Frederick.

 Rosalind. My father lov'd Sir Rowland as his soul,
And all the world was of my father's mind.
Had I before known this young man his son,[1]
I should have given him tears unto entreaties,
Ere he should thus have ventur'd.

 Celia.   Gentle cousin,
Let us go thank him and encourage him.
My father's rough and envious[2] disposition
Sticks me at heart.—Sir, you have well deserv'd.
If you do keep your promises in love
But justly, as you have exceeded promise,
Your mistress shall be happy.

 Rosalind.   Gentleman,

    [*Giving him a chain from her neck.*

Wear this for me, one out of suits with fortune,[3]
That could give more, but that her hand lacks means.—
Shall we go, coz?

 Celia.   Ay.—Fare you well, fair gentleman.

 Orlando. Can I not say, I thank you? My better parts
Are all thrown down, and that which here stands up
Is but a quintain,[4] a mere lifeless block.

 Rosalind. He calls us back: my pride fell with my fortunes;

---

[1] "His son," i.e., to be his son. [2] Malicious.

[3] "Out of suits with fortune," i.e., in misfortune.

[4] A quintain was a post with a crossbeam—afterwards the image of a

I'll ask him what he would.—Did you call, sir ?
Sir, you have wrestled well and overthrown
More than your enemies.
 Celia.   Will you go, coz ?
 Rosalind. Have with you.[1]—Fare you well.
       [Exeunt Rosalind and Celia.

 Orlando. What passion hangs these weights upon my tongue ?
I cannot speak to her, yet she urg'd conference.
O poor Orlando, thou art overthrown !
Or Charles or something weaker masters thee.

     Reënter LE BEAU.

 Le Beau. Good sir, I do in friendship counsel you
To leave this place. Albeit you have deserv'd
High commendation, true applause and love,
Yet such is now the Duke's condition [2]
That he misconstrues all that you have done.
The Duke is humorous;[3] what he is, indeed,
More suits you to conceive than I to speak of.

 Orlando. I thank you, sir; and, pray you, tell me this:
Which of the two was daughter of the Duke
That here was at the wrestling ?

 Le Beau. Neither his daughter, if we judge by manners;
But yet, indeed, the smaller is his daughter.
The other is daughter to the banish'd Duke,
And here detain'd by her usurping uncle,
To keep his daughter company; whose loves
Are dearer than the natural bond of sisters.
But I can tell you that of late this Duke
Hath ta'en displeasure 'gainst his gentle niece,

man—set in a pivot, and used as a target in military exercises. If the lance
of the horseman when tilting was awkwardly aimed, it might cause the figure
to turn and give the assailant a stroke with its projecting arm, thus dis-
gracing him.

 [1] " Have with you," i.e., I'll be with you. A common idiom.
 [2] Disposition.   [3] Capricious.

Grounded upon no other argument [1]
But that the people praise her for her virtues,
And pity her for her good father's sake;
And, on my life, his malice 'gainst the lady
Will suddenly [2] break forth.   Sir, fare you well.
Hereafter, in a better world than this, [3]
I shall desire more love and knowledge of you.

    Orlando. I rest much bounden to you.   Fare you well.

                                     [*Exit Le Beau.*

Thus must I from the smoke into the smother; [4]
From tyrant Duke unto a tyrant brother ; —
But heavenly Rosalind !   [*Exit.*

SCENE III.   *A Room in the Palace.*

Enter CELIA *and* ROSALIND.

    Celia. Why, cousin ! why, Rosalind ! Cupid have mercy !
not a word ?

    Rosalind. Not one to throw at a dog.

    Celia. No, thy words are too precious to be cast away upon
curs ; throw some of them at me ; come, lame me with reasons.

    Rosalind. Then there were two cousins laid up, when the one
should be lam'd with reasons and the other mad without any.

    Celia. But is all this for your father ?

    Rosalind. No, some of it is for my father's child.   O, how
full of briers is this working-day world !

    Celia. They are but burs, cousin, thrown upon thee in holiday
foolery.   If we walk not in the trodden paths, our very petticoats
will catch them.

    Rosalind. I could shake them off my coat; these burs are in
my heart.

    Celia. Hem [5] them away.

---

[1] Reason.   [2] Speedily; quickly.
[3] Le Beau means to say, "When things are in a better state than now."
[4] " From the smoke," etc., i.e., from bad to worse.   [5] Cough.

Rosalind. I would try, if I could cry " hem " and have him.

Celia. Come, come, wrestle with thy affections.

Rosalind. O, they take the part of a better wrestler than myself !

Celia. O, a good wish upon you ! you will try in time in spite of a fall. But, turning these jests out of service, let us talk in good earnest. Is it possible, on such a sudden, you should fall into so strong a liking with old Sir Rowland's youngest son ?

Rosalind. The Duke my father lov'd his father dearly.

Celia. Doth it therefore ensue that you should love his son dearly ? By this kind of chase [1] I should hate him, for my father hated his father dearly; [2] yet I hate not Orlando.

Rosalind. No, faith, hate him not, for my sake.

Celia. Why should I not ? doth he not deserve well ?

Rosalind. Let me love him for that, and do you love him because I do. Look, here comes the Duke.

Celia. With his eyes full of anger.

Enter DUKE FREDERICK, *with* Lords.

Duke F. Mistress, dispatch you with your safest haste,
And get you from our court.

Rosalind.   Me,[3] uncle ?

Duke F.   You, cousin.
Within these ten days if that thou be'st found
So near our public court as twenty miles,
Thou diest for it.

Rosalind.   I do beseech your grace,
Let me the knowledge of my fault bear with me.
If with myself I hold intelligence,
Or have acquaintance with mine own desires;
If that I do not dream or be not frantic,—

---

[1] " This kind of chase," i.e., this line of reasoning.

[2] Shakespeare uses " dear " of " whatever touches us nearly, either in love or hate, joy or sorrow."   [3] I.

As I do trust I am not,—then, dear uncle,
Never so much as in a thought unborn
Did I offend your highness.
    Duke F.   Thus do all traitors;
If their purgation [1] did consist in words,
They are as innocent as grace itself.
Let it suffice thee that I trust thee not.
    Rosalind. Yet your mistrust cannot make me a traitor.
Tell me whereon the likelihood depends.
    Duke F. Thou art thy father's daughter—there's enough.
    Rosalind. So was I when your highness took his dukedom;
So was I when your highness banish'd him.
Treason is not inherited, my lord;
Or, if we did derive it from our friends,
What's that to me ? my father was no traitor.
Then, good my liege, mistake me not so much
To think my poverty is treacherous.
    Celia. Dear sovereign, hear me speak.
    Duke F. Ay, Celia; we stay'd her for your sake,
Else had she with her father rang'd along.
    Celia. I did not then entreat to have her stay;
It was your pleasure and your own remorse.[2]
I was too young that time to value her;
But now I know her.   If she be a traitor,
Why, so am I; we still have slept together,
Rose at an instant, learn'd, play'd, eat together,
And wheresoe'er we went, like Juno's swans,[3]
Still we went coupled and inseparable.
    Duke F. She is too subtle for thee; and her smoothness,
Her very silence, and her patience
Speak to the people, and they pity her.

---

  [1] Clearance from guilt.   [2] Tenderness of heart.

  [3] " Juno's swans," i.e., the swans that drew the goddess's chariot.   But
the mythologists tell us the swan was sacred to Venus, and that Juno's car
was drawn by peacocks.

Thou art a fool; she robs thee of thy name,
And thou wilt show more bright and seem more virtuous
When she is gone. Then open not thy lips.
Firm and irrevocable is my doom
Which I have pass'd upon her: she is banish'd.

Celia. Pronounce that sentence then on me, my liege;
I cannot live out of her company.

Duke F. You are a fool!—You, niece, provide yourself.
If you outstay the time, upon mine honor,
And in the greatness of my word, you die.

              [Exeunt Duke Frederick and Lords.

Celia. O my poor Rosalind, whither wilt thou go?
Wilt thou change fathers? I will give thee mine.
I charge thee, be not thou more griev'd than I am.

Rosalind. I have more cause.

Celia.   Thou hast not, cousin;
Prithee, be cheerful. Know'st thou not the Duke
Hath banish'd me, his daughter?

Rosalind.   That he hath not.

Celia. No? hath not? Rosalind lacks then the love
Which teacheth thee that thou and I am[1] one.
Shall we be sunder'd? shall we part, sweet girl?
No: let my father seek another heir.
Therefore devise with me how we may fly,
Whither to go, and what to bear with us;
And do not seek to take the charge upon you,
To bear your griefs yourself and leave me out;
For, by this heaven, now at our sorrows pale,
Say what thou canst, I'll go along with thee.

Rosalind. Why, whither shall we go?

Celia. To seek my uncle in the Forest of Arden.

Rosalind. Alas, what danger will it be to us,
Maids as we are, to travel forth so far!
Beauty provoketh thieves sooner than gold.

                             [1] Are.

Celia. I'll put myself in poor and mean attire,
And with a kind of umber smirch my face;
The like do you; so shall we pass along
And never stir assailants.

   Rosalind.   Were it not better,
Because that I am more than common tall,
That I did suit me all points like a man?
A gallant curtle ax[1] upon my thigh,
A boar spear in my hand; and—in my heart
Lie there what hidden woman's fear there will—
We'll have a swashing[2] and a martial outside,
As many other mannish cowards have
That do outface it with their semblances.

   Celia. What shall I call thee when thou art a man?

   Rosalind. I'll have no worse a name than Jove's own page;
And therefore look you call me Ganymede.[3]
But what will you be call'd?

   Celia. Something that hath a reference to my state:
No longer Celia, but Aliena.

   Rosalind. But, cousin, what if we assay'd to steal
The clownish fool out of your father's court?
Would he not be a comfort to our travel?

   Celia. He'll go along o'er the wide world with me;
Leave me alone to woo[4] him.   Let's away,
And get our jewels and our wealth together,
Devise the fittest time and safest way
To hide us from pursuit that will be made
After my flight.   Now go we in content
To liberty and not to banishment.   [*Exeunt.*

---

   [1] "Curtle ax," i.e., a short sword. The name is a corruption of "cutlass."   [2] Swaggering.

   [3] A beautiful youth of Phrygia, son of Tros, who, while feeding his father's flocks on Mount Ida, was taken up to Olympus by Jupiter, and became the cupbearer of the gods.   [4] Persuade; gain over.

ACT II.

Scene I. *The Forest of Arden.*

Enter Duke Senior, Amiens, *and two or three* Lords, *like foresters.*

Duke S. Now, my co-mates and brothers in exile',
Hath not old custom made this life more sweet
Than that of painted pomp? Are not these woods
More free from peril than the envious court?
Here feel we but the penalty of Adam, —
The seasons' difference, as the icy fang
And churlish chiding of the winter's wind,
Which, when it bites and blows upon my body,
Even till I shrink with cold, I smile and say,
"This is no flattery; these are counselors
That feelingly persuade me what I am."
Sweet are the uses of adversity,
Which, like the toad, ugly and venomous,
Wears yet a precious jewel in his head; [1]
And this our life, exempt from public haunt,
Finds tongues in trees, books in the running brooks,
Sermons in stones, and good in everything.
I would not change it.
    Amiens.   Happy is your grace,
That can translate the stubbornness of fortune
Into so quiet and so sweet a style.
    Duke S. Come, shall we go and kill us venison?
And yet it irks [2] me the poor dappled fools,
Being native burghers [3] of this desert city,

---

[1] That the toad was venomous, and that it had a precious jewel in its head, were old superstitions in Shakespeare's day. The toadstone was supposed to be an antidote for poison.

[2] Distresses.   [3] Citizens.

Should in their own confines', with forked heads [1]
Have their round haunches gor'd.
    First Lord.   Indeed, my lord,
The melancholy Jaques grieves at that,
And, in that kind,[2] swears you do more usurp
Than doth your brother that hath banish'd you.
To-day my Lord of Amiens and myself
Did steal behind him as he lay along
Under an oak whose an'tique root peeps out
Upon the brook that brawls along this wood.
To the which place a poor sequester'd [3] stag,
That from the hunter's aim had ta'en a hurt,
Did come to languish; and indeed, my lord,
The wretched animal heav'd forth such groans
That their discharge did stretch his leathern coat
Almost to bursting, and the big round tears
Cours'd one another down his innocent nose
In piteous chase; and thus the hairy fool,
Much marked of the melancholy Jaques,
Stood on the extremest verge of the swift brook,
Augmenting it with tears.
    Duke S.   But what said Jaques?
Did he not moralize this spectacle?
    First Lord. O yes, into a thousand similes.
First, for his weeping into the needless stream: [4]
" Poor deer," quoth he, "thou mak'st a testament
As worldlings do, giving thy sum of more
To that which had too much." Then, being there alone,
Left and abandon'd of his velvet [5] friends,
" 'Tis right," quoth he; "thus misery doth part
The flux [6] of company." Anon a careless herd,

---

[1] Arrowheads.   [2] Way.
[3] Separated from the herd.
[4] " Needless stream," i.e., a stream that already had water enough.
[5] Sleek; prosperous.   [6] Coming together.

Full of the pasture, jumps along by him
And never stays to greet him.   "Ay," quoth Jaques,
" Sweep on, you fat and greasy citizens ;
'Tis just the fashion ; wherefore do you look
Upon that poor and broken bankrupt there ? "
Thus most invectively he pierceth through   •
The body of the country, city, court, —
Yea, and of this our life, swearing that we
Are mere usurpers, tyrants, and what's worse,
To fright the animals and to kill them up [1]
In their assign'd and native dwelling place.

   Duke S. And did you leave him in this contemplation ?

   Second Lord. We did, my lord, weeping and commenting
Upon the sobbing deer.

   Duke S.   Show me the place.
I love to cope [2] him in these sullen fits,
For then he's full of matter. [3]

   First Lord. I'll bring you to him straight. [4]   [*Exeunt.*

SCENE II.   *A Room in the Palace.*

Enter DUKE FREDERICK, *with* Lords.

   Duke F. Can it be possible that no man saw them ?
It cannot be ; some villains of my court
Are of consent and sufferance in this. [5]

   First Lord. I cannot hear of any that did see her.
The ladies, her attendants of her chamber,
Saw her abed, and in the morning early
They found the bed untreasur'd of their mistress.

   Second Lord. My lord, the roynish [6] clown, at whom so oft
Your grace was wont to laugh, is also missing.

---

[1] " Kill them up ; " we should say now, " kill them off."
[2] Meet with.   [3] Sound sense.   [4] Immediately.
[5] " Are of consent," etc., i.e., knew of this escape and connived at it.
[6] Rascally.

Hisperia, the princess' gentlewoman,
Confesses that she secretly o'erheard
Your daughter and her cousin much commend
The parts and graces of the wrestler
That did but lately foil the sinewy Charles;
And she believes, wherever they are gone,
That youth is surely in their company.

 Duke F. Send to his brother; fetch that gallant hither.
If he be absent, bring his brother to me;
I'll make him find him. Do this suddenly,
And let not search and inquisition quail [1]
To bring again these foolish runaways.   [*Exeunt.*

SCENE III. Before Oliver's House.

Enter ORLANDO and ADAM, meeting.

 Orlando. Who's there?

 Adam. What! my young master? O my gentle master!
O my sweet master! O you memory
Of old Sir Rowland! why, what make you here?
Why are you virtuous? why do people love you?
And wherefore are you gentle, strong, and valiant?
Why would you be so fond [2] to overcome
The bonny priser [3] of the humorous [4] Duke?
Your praise is come too swiftly home before you.
Know you not, master, to some kind of men
Their graces serve them but as enemies?
No more do yours; your virtues, gentle master,
Are sanctified and holy traitors to you.
O, what a world is this, when what is comely
Envenoms him that bears it!

 Orlando. Why, what's the matter?

 Adam.   O unhappy youth!

---

1 " Inquisition quail," i.e., inquiry slacken.   2 Foolish.
3 " Bonny priser," i.e., gallant prize fighter.   4 See Note 3, p. 28.

Come not within these doors; within this roof
The enemy of all your graces lives.
Your brother — no, no brother, yet the son —
Yet not the son; I will not call him son
Of him I was about to call his father —
Hath heard your praises, and this night he means
To burn the lodging where you use to lie,[1]
And you within it; if he fail of that,
He will have other means to cut you off.
I overheard him and his practices.[2]
This is no place;[3] this house is but a butchery.[4]
Abhor it, fear it, do not enter it!

   Orlando. Why, whither, Adam, wouldst thou have me go ?
   Adam. No matter whither, so you come not here.
   Orlando. What, wouldst thou have me go and beg my food ?
Or with a base and boisterous sword enforce
A thievish living on the common road ?
This I must do, or know not what to do;
Yet this I will not do, do how I can.
I rather will subject me to the malice
Of a diverted blood and bloody brother.[5]

   Adam. But do not so. I have five hundred crowns,
The thrifty hire I sav'd under your father,
Which I did store to be my foster nurse
When service should in my old limbs lie lame,
And unregarded age in corners thrown.
Take that; and He that doth the ravens feed,
Yea, providently caters for the sparrow,[6]
Be comfort to my age ! Here is the gold;

---

[1] " Use to lie," i.e., it is your custom to sleep.
[2] Evil designs.   [3] Fit dwelling.
[4] Here used in the sense of " slaughterhouse."
[5] " Malice of," etc., i.e., the alienated natural affection of a murderous brother.
[6] See Ps. cxlvii. 9, and Luke xii. 6.

All this I give you.   Let me be your servant.
Though I look old, yet I am strong and lusty;
For in my youth I never did apply
Hot and rebellious liquors in my blood,
Nor did not with unbashful forehead woo
The means of weakness and debility;
Therefore my age is as a lusty winter,
Frosty, but kindly.[1]   Let me go with you;
I'll do the service of a younger man
In all your business and necessities.

   Orlando. O good old man, how well in thee appears
The constant[2] service of the an'tique world,
When service sweat for duty, not for meed![3]
Thou art not for the fashion of these times,
Where none will sweat but for promotion,
And having that, do choke their service up
Even with the having;[4] it is not so with thee.
But, poor old man, thou prun'st a rotten tree,
That cannot so much as a blossom yield
In lieu[5] of all thy pains and husbandry.
But come thy ways; we'll go along together,
And ere we have thy youthful wages spent,
We'll light upon some settled low content.

   Adam. Master, go on, and I will follow thee,
To the last gasp, with truth and loyalty. —
From seventeen years till now almost fourscore
Here lived I, but now live here no more.
At seventeen years many their fortunes seek;
But at fourscore it is too late a week.[6]
Yet fortune cannot recompense me better
Than to die well and not my master's debtor.   [*Exeunt.*

---

1 Natural; hence, healthy.   2 Faithful.   3 Reward.

4 Because of their promotion they become too proud to serve.

5 "In lieu," i.e., in return for.

6 "Too late a week," i.e., too late in the week; much too late.

SCENE IV. *The Forest of Arden.*

Enter ROSALIND *for* GANYMEDE, CELIA *for* ALIENA, *and* TOUCHSTONE.

Rosalind. O Jupiter, how weary are my spirits!

Touchstone. I care not for my spirits, if my legs were not weary.

Rosalind. I could find in my heart to disgrace my man's apparel and to cry like a woman; but I must comfort the weaker vessel, as doublet and hose [1] ought to show itself courageous to petticoat; therefore courage, good Aliena!

Celia. I pray you, bear with me; I cannot go no [2] further.

Touchstone. For my part, I had rather bear with you than bear you; yet I should bear no cross [3] if I did bear you, for I think you have no money in your purse.

Rosalind. Well, this is the Forest of Arden.

Touchstone. Ay, now am I in Arden — the more fool I! When I was at home I was in a better place; but travelers must be content.

Rosalind. Ay, be so, good Touchstone.

Enter CORIN *and* SILVIUS.

Look you, who comes here? a young man and an old in solemn [4] talk.

Corin. That is the way to make her scorn you still.

Silvius. O Corin, that thou knew'st how I do love her!

---

[1] "Doublet and hose," i.e., coat and breeches. "The doublet was close and fitted tightly to the body, the skirts reaching a little below the girdle. The word 'hose,' now applied solely to the stocking, was used originally to imply the breeches" or tight trousers.

[2] Double negatives are frequent in Shakespeare.

[3] A cross is a heavy burden, figuratively. The penny of Queen Elizabeth was stamped with a cross, and was familiarly so called. Touchstone puns on the two meanings.

[4] Serious; earnest.

Corin. I partly guess ; for I have lov'd ere now.

Silvius. No, Corin, being old, thou canst not guess,
Though in thy youth thou wast as true a lover
As ever sigh'd upon a midnight pillow.
But if thy love were ever like to mine, —
As sure I think did never man love so, —
How many actions most ridiculous
Hast thou been drawn to by thy fantasy ? [1]

Corin. Into a thousand that I have forgotten.

Silvius. O, thou didst then ne'er love so heartily !
If thou remember'st not the slightest folly
That ever love did make thee run into,
Thou hast not lov'd ;
Or if thou hast not sat as I do now,
Wearing thy hearer in thy mistress' praise,
Thou hast not lov'd ;
Or if thou hast not broke from company
Abruptly, as my passion now makes me,
Thou hast not lov'd.
O Phebe, Phebe, Phebe !   [*Exit.*

Rosalind. Alas, poor shepherd ! searching of thy wound,
I have by hard adventure found mine own.

Touchstone. And I mine. I remember, when I was in love, I
broke my sword upon a stone and bid him take that for coming
a-night to Jane Smile ; and I remember the kissing of her batlet [2]
and the cow's dugs that her pretty chopt hands had milk'd ; and
I remember the wooing of a peascod instead of her, from whom
I took two cods and, giving her them again, said with weeping
tears, " Wear these for my sake." [3]   We that are true lovers run

---

[1] Fancy; i.e., love.   [2] A little bat used by laundresses.

[3] " Our [English] ancestors were frequently accustomed in their love
affairs to employ the divination of a peascod [pea pod], by selecting one
growing on the stem, snatching it away quickly, and if the omen of the peas
remaining in the pod were preserved, then presenting it to the lady of their
choice." (BRAND'S *Popular Antiquities*, quoted by W. Aldis Wright.)

into strange capers; but as all is mortal in nature, so is all nature in love mortal in folly.[1]

Rosalind. Thou speakest wiser than thou art 'ware of.

Touchstone. Nay, I shall ne'er be 'ware of mine own wit till I break my shins against it.

Rosalind. Jove, Jove ! this shepherd's passion
Is much upon my fashion.

Touchstone. And mine; but it grows something stale with me.

Celia. I pray you, one of you question yond man
If he for gold will give us any food.
I faint almost to death.

Touchstone. Holla, you clown !

Rosalind. Peace, fool; he's not thy kinsman.

Corin. Who calls ?

Touchstone. Your betters, sir.

Corin. Else are they very wretched.

Rosalind. Peace, I say.—Good even to you, friend.

Corin. And to you, gentle sir, and to you all.

Rosalind. I prithee, shepherd, if that love or gold
Can in this desert place buy entertainment,
Bring us where we may rest ourselves and feed.
Here's a young maid with travel much oppress'd,
And faints for succor.

Corin. • Fair sir, I pity her,
And wish, for her sake more than for mine own,
My fortunes were more able to relieve her;
But I am shepherd to another man,
And do not shear the fleeces that I graze.
My master is of churlish disposition,
And little recks[2] to find the way to heaven
By doing deeds of hospitality.
Besides, his cote,[3] his flocks, and bounds of feed
Are now on sale, and at our sheepcote now,

---

[1] " Mortal in folly," i.e., extremely foolish.
[2] Cares.   [3] Hut.

By reason of his absence, there is nothing
That you will feed on; but what is, come see,
And in my voice most welcome shall you be.

    Rosalind. What is he that shall buy his flock and pasture?

    Corin. That young swain that you saw here but erewhile,[1]
That little cares for buying anything.

    Rosalind. I pray thee, if it stand with honesty,
Buy thou the cottage, pasture, and the flock,
And thou shalt have to pay for it of us.

    Celia. And we will mend thy wages. I like this place,
And willingly could waste[2] my time in it.

    Corin. Assuredly the thing is to be sold.
Go with me; if you like upon report
The soil, the profit, and this kind of life,
I will your very faithful feeder[3] be,
And buy it with your gold right suddenly.   [*Exeunt.*

Scene V. *The Forest.*

Enter AMIENS, JAQUES, *and others.*

Song.

Amiens.
    Under the greenwood tree
    Who loves to lie with me,
    And turn his merry note
    Unto the sweet bird's throat,
Come hither, come hither, come hither;
    Here shall he see
    No enemy
But winter and rough weather.

    Jaques. More, more, I prithee, more!

    Amiens. It will make you melancholy, Monsieur Jaques.

    Jaques. I thank it. More, I prithee, more! I can suck melancholy out of a song, as a weasel sucks eggs. More, I prithee, more!

---

[1] Just now.   [2] Spend.   [3] Servant.

Amiens. My voice is ragged; I know I cannot please you.

Jaques. I do not desire you to please me; I do desire you to sing. Come, more; another stanzo; call you 'em stanzos?

Amiens. What you will, Monsieur Jaques.

Jaques. Nay, I care not for their names; they owe me nothing. Will you sing?

Amiens. More at your request than to please myself.

Jaques. Well, then, if ever I thank any man, I'll thank you; but that they call compliment is like the encounter of two dog apes, and when a man thanks me heartily, methinks I have given him a penny and he renders me the beggarly thanks. Come, sing;—and you that will not, hold your tongues.

Amiens. Well, I'll end the song.—Sirs, cover[1] the while; the Duke will drink under this tree.—He hath been all this day to look[2] you.

Jaques. And I have been all this day to avoid him. He is too disputable[3] for my company. I think of as many matters as he, but I give Heaven thanks, and make no boast of them. Come, warble, come!

SONG.

> *Who doth ambition shun,*   [*All together here.*
> *And loves to live i' th' sun,*
> *Seeking the food he eats*
> *And pleas'd with what he gets,*
> *Come hither, come hither, come hither;*
> *Here shall he see*
> *No enemy*
> *But winter and rough weather.*

Jaques. I'll give you a verse to this note that I made yesterday in despite of my invention.[4]

---

[1] Prepare the table for the banquet.   [2] Look for.
[3] Fond of argument.
[4] "In despite of my invention," i.e., though my imagination gave its help unwillingly.

Amiens. And I'll sing it.

Jaques. Thus it goes:

> *If it do come to pass*
> *That any man turn ass,*
> *Leaving his wealth and ease,*
> *A stubborn will to please,*
> *Ducdàme, ducdàme, ducdàme ;*
> *Here shall he see*
> *Gross fools as he,*
> *An if he will come to me.*

Amiens. What's that " ducdàme ? "

Jaques. 'Tis a Greek invocation, to call fools into a circle. I'll go sleep, if I can; if I cannot, I'll rail against all the first-born of Egypt.[1]

Amiens. And I'll go seek the Duke ; his banquet is prepared.

[*Exeunt severally.*

SCENE VI.   *The Forest.*

Enter ORLANDO *and* ADAM.

Adam. Dear master, I can go no further. O, I die for food ! Here lie I down, and measure out my grave. Farewell, kind master.

Orlando. Why, how now, Adam ! no greater heart in thee ? Live a little ; comfort a little ; cheer thyself a little. If this un-couth forest yield anything savage, I will either be food for it or bring it for food to thee. Thy conceit[2] is nearer death than thy powers. For my sake be comfortable ; hold death awhile at the arm's end. I will here be with thee presently ; and if I bring thee not something to eat, I will give thee leave to die ; but if thou diest before I come, thou art a mocker of my labor. Well said ! thou look'st cheerly,[3] and I'll be with thee quickly. Yet thou liest

---

[1] Dr. Johnson notes that the expression " firstborn of Egypt " was a proverbial one for highborn persons.

[2] Imagination.   [3] Cheerfully.

in the bleak air. Come, I will bear thee to some shelter; and thou
shalt not die for lack of a dinner, if there live anything in this
desert. Cheerly, good Adam! [*Exeunt.*

Scene VII. *The Forest.*

A table set out. Enter Duke Senior, Amiens, *and* Lords *like outlaws.*

Duke S. I think he be transform'd into a beast;
For I can nowhere find him like a man.
First Lord. My lord, he is but even now gone hence;
Here was he merry, hearing of a song.
Duke S. If he, compact of jars,[1] grow musical,
We shall have shortly discord in the spheres.[2]
Go, seek him; tell him I would speak with him.

Enter Jaques.

First Lord. He saves my labor by his own approach.
Duke S. Why, how now, monsieur! what a life is this,
That your poor friends must woo your company?
What, you look merrily!
Jaques. A fool, a fool! I met a fool i' the forest,
A motley[3] fool!—A miserable world!—
As I do live by food, I met a fool,
Who laid him down and bask'd him in the sun,
And rail'd on Lady Fortune in good terms,
In good set terms, and yet a motley fool.
"Good morrow, fool," quoth I. "No, sir," quoth he,
"Call me not fool till Heaven hath sent me fortune."
And then he drew a dial from his poke,[4]

---

[1] "Compact of jars," i.e., made up of discords.
[2] The doctrine of Pythagoras that the heavenly bodies in their motion
produce harmonious sounds, is frequently referred to by Shakespeare.
[3] Party-colored. The dress of the professional fool, who had a place in
every large household, was patched with various colors.
[4] Pocket.

And, looking on it with lackluster eye,
Says very wisely, " It is ten o'clock.
Thus we may see," quoth he, " how the world wags;
'Tis but an hour ago since it was nine,
And after one hour more 'twill be eleven ;
And so, from hour to hour, we ripe and ripe,
And then, from hour to hour, we rot and rot;
And thereby hangs a tale." .When I did hear
The motley fool thus moral [1] on the time,
My lungs began to crow like chanticleer,
That fools should be so deep-contemplative,
And I did laugh sans [2] intermission
An hour by his dial.   O noble fool !
O worthy fool !   Motley's the only wear.[3]
    Duke S. What fool is this ?
    Jaques. A worthy fool !   One that hath been a courtier,
And says, if ladies be but young and fair,
They have the gift to know it ; and in his brain,
Which is as dry as the remainder biscuit
After a voyage, he hath strange places cramm'd
With observation, the which he vents
In mangled forms.   O that I were a fool !
I am ambitious for a motley coat.
    Duke S. Thou shalt have one.
    Jaques.   It is my only suit,[4]
Provided that you weed your better judgments
Of all opinion that grows rank in them
That I am wise.   I must have liberty
Withal, as large a charter as the wind,
To blow on whom I please ; for so fools have ;
And they that are most galled with my folly,
They most must laugh.   And why, sir, must they so ?

---

[1] Moralize.   [2] A French word meaning " without."
[3] " Motley's the only wear," i.e., there is no dress like the fool's.
[4] A play upon the word is doubtless intended.

The " why " is plain as way to parish church:
He that a fool doth very wisely hit,
Doth very foolishly, although he smart,
But to seem senseless of the bob;[1] if not,
The wise man's folly is anatomiz'd
Even by the squandering glances[2] of the fool.
Invest me in my motley; give me leave
To speak my mind, and I will through and through
Cleanse the foul body of the infected world,
If they will patiently receive my medicine.

    Duke S. Fie on thee ! I can tell what thou wouldst do.

    Jaques. What, for a counter,[3] would I do but good ?

    Duke S. Most mischievous foul sin, in chiding sin;
For thou thyself hast been a libertine,
As sensual as the brutish sting itself;
And all the embossed sores and headed evils,
That thou with license of free foot hast caught,
Wouldst thou disgorge into the general world.

    Jaques. Why, who cries out on pride,
That can therein tax[4] any private party ?
Doth it not flow as hugely as the sea,
Till that the wearer's very means do ebb ?
What woman in the city do I name,
When that I say the city woman bears
The cost of princes on unworthy shoulders ?
Who can come in and say that I mean her,
When such a one as she, such is her neighbor ?
Or what is he of basest function,[5]
That says his bravery is not on my cost,[6]
Thinking that I mean him, but therein suits

---

[1] Blow.

[2] " Squandering glances," i.e., gibes scattered without special aim.

[3] " For a counter," i.e., on the wager of a counter. The counter was a worthless coin, used only for calculations.

[4] Censure.   [5] Occupation.

[6] " His bravery," etc., i.e., his fine clothes are not at my expense.

His folly to the mettle of my speech?
There then; how then? what then?   Let me see wherein
My tongue hath wrong'd him.   If it do him right,
Then he hath wrong'd himself; if he be free,
Why then my taxing like a wild goose flies,
Unclaim'd of any man.— But who comes here?

Enter ORLANDO, *with his sword drawn.*

Orlando.   Forbear, and eat no more.
Jaques.   Why, I have eat none yet.
Orlando.   Nor shalt not, till necessity be serv'd.
Jaques.   Of what kind should this cock come of? [1]
Duke S.   Art thou thus bolden'd, man, by thy distress,
Or else a rude despiser of good manners,
That in civility thou seem'st so empty?
Orlando.   You touch'd my vein at first; the thorny point
Of bare distress hath ta'en from me the show
Of smooth civility; yet am I inland bred, [2]
And know some nurture. [3]   But forbear, I say!
He dies that touches any of this fruit
Till I and my affairs are answered.
Jaques.   An you will not be answered with reason, I must
      die.
Duke S.   What would you have?   Your gentleness shall
      force
More than your force move us to gentleness.
Orlando.   I almost die for food; and let me have it.
Duke S.   Sit down and feed, and welcome to our table.
Orlando.   Speak you so gently?   Pardon me, I pray you;
I thought that all things had been savage here,
And therefore put I on the countenance
Of stern commandment.   But whate'er you are

---

[1] This repeating of the preposition is often met with in Shakespeare.
[2] " Inland bred," i.e., not a rustic brought up on the frontier.
[3] Good breeding.

   4

That in this desert inaccessible,
Under the shade of melancholy boughs,
Lose and neglect the creeping hours of time;
If ever you have look'd on better days,
If ever been where bells have knoll'd to church,
If ever sat at any good man's feast,
If ever from your eyelids wip'd a tear,
And know what 'tis to pity and be pitied, —
Let gentleness my strong enforcement be;
In the which hope I blush, and hide my sword.
  Duke S. True is it that we have seen better days,
And have with holy bell been knoll'd to church,
And sat at good men's feasts, and wip'd our eyes
Of drops that sacred pity hath engender'd;
And therefore sit you down in gentleness,
And take upon command what help we have
That to your wanting may be minister'd.
  Orlando. Then but forbear your food a little while,
Whiles like a doe I go to find my fawn
And give it food. There is an old poor man,
Who after me hath many a weary step
Limp'd in pure love; till he be first suffic'd, —
Oppress'd with two weak evils,[1] age and hunger, —
I will not touch a bit.
  Duke S.   Go find him out,
And we will nothing waste till you return.
  Orlando. I thank ye; and be blest for your good comfort!
                                          |Exit.

  Duke S. Thou seest we are not all alone unhappy.
This wide and universal theater
Presents more woful pageants than the scene
Wherein we play in.
  Jaques.   All the world's a stage,
And all the men and women merely players.

----

1 " Weak evils," i.e., evils causing weakness.

They have their exits and their entrances;
And one man in his time plays many parts,
His acts being seven ages.   At first the infant,
Mewling and puking in the nurse's arms.
And then the whining schoolboy, with his satchel
And shining morning face, creeping like snail
Unwillingly to school.   And then the lover,
Sighing like furnace, with a woful ballad
Made to his mistress' eyebrow.   Then a soldier,
Full of strange oaths and bearded like the pard;[1]
Jealous in honor, sudden and quick in quarrel,
Seeking the bubble reputation
Even in the cannon's mouth.   And then the justice,
In fair round belly with good capon lin'd,
With eyes severe and beard of formal cut,
Full of wise saws and modern instances;[2]
And so he plays his part.   The sixth age shifts
Into the lean and slipper'd pantaloon,[3]
With spectacles on nose and pouch on side,
His youthful hose, well sav'd, a world too wide
For his shrunk shank; and his big manly voice,
Turning again toward childish treble, pipes
And whistles in his[4] sound.   Last scene of all,
That ends this strange, eventful history,
Is second childishness and mere oblivion,
Sans teeth, sans eyes, sans taste, sans everything.

Reënter ORLANDO *with* ADAM.

Duke S. Welcome.   Set down your venerable burden,
And let him feed.

---

[1] " Bearded like the pard," i.e., with long, pointed mustaches like the leopard's feelers.

[2] " Full of wise saws," etc., i.e., crammed with wise sayings and commonplace illustrations.

[3] The name of a comic character in Italian plays.

[4] The pronoun " its " was rarely used in Shakespeare's day.

Orlando. I thank you most for him.

Adam.   So had you need;—
I scarce can speak to thank you for myself.

Duke S. Welcome; fall to.   I will not trouble you,
As yet, to question you about your fortunes.—
Give us some music; and, good cousin, sing.

SONG.

Amiens.   *Blow, blow, thou winter wind,*
                 Thou art not so unkind
                     As man's ingratitude;
                 Thy tooth is not so keen,
                 Because thou art not seen,
                     Although thy breath be rude.
Heigh-ho! sing, heigh-ho! unto the green holly!
Most friendship is feigning, most loving mere folly;
             Then, heigh-ho, the holly!
             This life is most jolly.

                 Freeze, freeze, thou bitter sky,
                 That dost not bite so nigh
                     As benefits forgot:
                 Though thou the waters warp,
                 Thy sting is not so sharp
                     As friend remember'd not.[1]
Heigh-ho! sing, etc.

Duke S. If that you were the good Sir Rowland's son,
As you have whisper'd faithfully you were,
And as mine eye doth his effigies witness
Most truly limn'd and living in your face,
Be truly welcome hither.   I am the Duke
That lov'd your father; the residue of your fortune,
Go to my cave and tell me.—Good old man,
Thou art right welcome as thy master is.—
Support him by the arm.—Give me your hand,
And let me all your fortunes understand.   [*Exeunt.*

---

[1] "As friend," etc., i.e., as what an unremembered friend feels.

ACT III.

SCENE I. *A Room in the Palace.*

Enter DUKE FREDERICK, Lords, *and* OLIVER.

Duke F. Not see him since ? Sir, sir, that cannot be ;
But were I not the better part made mercy,
I should not seek an absent argument [1]
Of my revenge, thou present. But look to it :
Find out thy brother, wheresoe'er he is ;
Seek him with candle ;[2] bring him dead or living
Within this twelvemonth, or turn thou no more
To seek a living in our territory.
Thy lands and all things which thou dost call thine,
Worth seizure, do we seize into our hands,
Till thou canst quit thee by thy brother's mouth
Of what we think against thee.

    Oliver. O that your highness knew my heart in this !
I never lov'd my brother in my life.

    Duke F. More villain thou. — Well, push him out of doors ;
And let my officers of such a nature
Make an extent [3] upon his house and lands.
Do this expediently,[4] and turn him going.   [*Exeunt.*

SCENE II. *The Forest.*

Enter ORLANDO, *with a paper.*

Orlando. Hang there, my verse, in witness of my love. —
    And thou, thrice-crowned Queen of Night,[5] survey

---

[1] Object.   [2] See Luke xv. 8.

[3] " Make an extent," i.e., seize by writ of attachment.

[4] Expeditiously.

[5] " Thrice-crowned Queen of Night," i.e., the moon ; known as Luna or Cynthia in heaven, Hecate or Proserpina in the lower regions, and on earth as Diana, who was also goddess of the chase and of chastity.

With thy chaste eye, from thy pale sphere above,
  Thy huntress' name that my full life doth sway.—
O Rosalind ! these trees shall be my books,
  And in their barks my thoughts I'll character;[1] ·
That every eye which in this forest looks,
  Shall see thy virtue witness'd everywhere.—
Run, run, Orlando; carve on every tree
The fair, the chaste, and unexpressive [2] she.   [*Exit.*

Enter CORIN *and* TOUCHSTONE.

Corin. And how like you this shepherd's life, Master Touchstone ?

Touchstone. Truly, shepherd, in respect of itself, it is a good
life; but in respect that it is a shepherd's life, it is naught.[3]   In
respect that it is solitary, I like it very well; but in respect that
it is private, it is a very vile life. Now, in respect it is in the
fields, it pleaseth me well; but in respect it is not in the court,
it is tedious. As it is a spare life, look you, it fits my humor
well; but as there is no more plenty in it, it goes much against
my stomach. Hast any philosophy in thee, shepherd ?

Corin. No more but that I know the more one sickens the
worse at ease he is, and that he that wants money, means, and
content is without three good friends; that the property of rain
is to wet, and fire to burn; that good pasture makes fat sheep,
and that a great cause of the night is lack of the sun; that he
that hath learned no wit by nature nor art may complain of good
breeding [4] or comes of a very dull kindred.

Touchstone. Such a one is a natural philosopher.—Wast ever
in court, shepherd ?

Corin. No, truly.

Touchstone. Then thou art damn'd.

Corin. Nay, I hope.

[1] Carve.   [2] Inexpressible.   [3] See Note 2, p. 22.
[4] " Complain," etc., i.e., complain of not having been well brought up.

Touchstone. Truly, thou art damn'd, like an ill-roasted egg all on one side.

Corin. For not being at court? Your reason.

Touchstone. Why, if thou never wast at court, thou never saw'st good manners; if thou never saw'st good manners, then thy manners must be wicked; and wickedness is sin, and sin is damnation. Thou art in a parlous [1] state, shepherd.

Corin. Not a whit, Touchstone; those that are good manners at the court are as ridiculous in the country as the behavior of the country is most mockable at the court. You told me you salute not at the court but you kiss [2] your hands; that courtesy would be uncleanly if courtiers were shepherds.

Touchstone. Instance,[3] briefly; come, instance.

Corin. Why, we are still [4] handling our ewes, and their fells,[5] you know, are greasy.

Touchstone. Why, do not your courtier's hands sweat? and is not the grease of a mutton as wholesome as the sweat of a man? Shallow, shallow. A better instance, I say; come.

Corin. Besides, our hands are hard.

Touchstone. Your lips will feel them the sooner. Shallow again. A more sounder [6] instance, come.

Corin. And they are often tarr'd over with the surgery of our sheep; and would you have us kiss tar? The courtier's hands are perfum'd with civet.[7]

Touchstone. Most shallow man! thou worms'-meat, in respect of a good piece of flesh indeed! Learn of the wise, and perpend:[8] civet is of a baser birth than tar. Mend the instance, shepherd.

Corin. You have too courtly a wit for me; I'll rest.

Touchstone. Wilt thou rest damn'd? God help thee, shallow man! God make incision in thee![9] thou art raw.

Corin. Sir, I am a true laborer. I earn that I eat, get that I

---

[1] Perilous.　　　[2] "But you kiss," i.e., without kissing.

[3] Give an example; prove it.　　　[4] Continually.　　　[5] Skins.

[6] Double comparatives are used by all Elizabethan writers.
　　A perfume derived from the civet cat.　　　[8] Consider.

[9] Alluding to the old practice of bloodletting as a cure for most diseases.

wear; owe no man hate, envy no man's happiness; glad of other men's good, content with my harm;[1] and the greatest of my pride is to see my ewes graze and my lambs suck. Here comes young Master Ganymede, my new mistress's brother.

Enter ROSALIND, *with a paper, reading.*

Rosalind. *From the east to western Ind,*
No jewel is like Rosalind.
Her worth, being mounted on the wind,
Through all the world bears Rosalind.
All the pictures fairest lin'd
Are but black to Rosalind.
Let no face be kept in mind
But the fair of Rosalind.

Touchstone. I'll rhyme you so eight years together, dinners and suppers and sleeping hours excepted; it is the right butter-women's rank[2] to market.

Rosalind. Out, fool!

Touchstone. For a taste:

If a hart do lack a hind,
Let him seek out Rosalind.
If the cat will after kind,
So be sure will Rosalind.
Winter garments must be lin'd,
So must slender Rosalind.
They that reap must sheaf and bind;
Then to cart with Rosalind.
Sweetest nut hath sourest rind,
Such a nut is Rosalind.
He that sweetest rose will find
Must find love's prick and Rosalind.

This is the very false gallop of verses; why do you infect your-self with them?

[1] "Content with my harm," i.e., bear my misfortunes patiently.
[2] "Going one after another at a jog trot."

Rosalind. Peace, you dull fool ! I found them on a tree.

Touchstone. Truly, the tree yields bad fruit.

Rosalind. I'll graff [1] it with you, and then I shall graff it with a medlar; [2] then it will be the earliest fruit i' the country; for you'll be rotten ere you be half ripe, and that's the right virtue of the medlar.

Touchstone. You have said; but whether wisely or no, let the forest judge.

Enter CELIA, *with a writing.*

Rosalind. Peace !
Here comes my sister, reading.   Stand aside.

Celia. [*Reads*]

> *Why should this a desert be ?*
> *For [3] it is unpeopled ?   No ;*
> *Tongues I'll hang on every tree,*
> *That shall civil sayings [4] show.*
> *Some, how brief the life of man*
> *Runs his erring [5] pilgrimage,*
> *That [6] the stretching of a span*
> *Buckles in his sum of age;*
> *Some, of violated vows*
> *'Twixt the souls of friend and friend.*
> *But upon the fairest boughs,*
> *Or at every sentence end,*
> *Will I Rosalinda write,*
> *Teaching all that read to know*
> *The quintessence of every sprite*
> *Heaven would in little show.*
> *Therefore Heaven Nature charg'd*
> *That one body should be fill'd*
> *With all graces wide-enlarg'd.*
> *Nature presently distill'd*

---

[1] Graft.

[2] A small European tree, the fruit of which, like that of the American persimmon, is not fit to be eaten till it is overripe.

[3] Because.   [4] " Civil sayings," i.e., sayings of civilized society.

[5] Errant; wandering.   [6] So that.

> *Helen's* [1] *cheek, but not her heart ;*
>   *Cleopatra's* [2] *majesty ;*
>   *Atalanta's better part ;* [3]
>   *Sad Lucretia's* [4] *modesty.*
> *Thus Rosalind of many parts*
>   *By heavenly synod was devis'd,*
> *Of many faces, eyes, and hearts,*
>   *To have the touches* [5] *dearest priz'd.*
> *Heaven would that she these gifts should have,*
> *And I to live and die her slave.*

Rosalind. O most gentle pulpiter ! what tedious homily of
love have you wearied your parishioners withal, and never cried,
"Have patience, good people"!

Celia. How now ! Back, friends !—Shepherd, go off a little.
—Go with him, sirrah.

Touchstone. Come, shepherd, let us make an honorable re-
treat; though not with bag and baggage, yet with scrip and
scrippage.   [*Exeunt Corin and Touchstone.*

Celia. Didst thou hear these verses ?

---

[1] Helen, according to classic mythology, was the daughter of Jupiter,
and the most beautiful woman of her time. Her treacherous desertion of
her husband, King Menelaus of Sparta, and her elopement with Paris, a
prince of Troy, occasioned the Trojan War, the theme of Homer's Iliad.

[2] Cleopatra, the celebrated Egyptian queen, famed in history and fiction
for her beauty and mental perfections, and for the wonderful fascination of her
coquetry, died in 30 B.C., after a reign of twenty-four years.

[3] "Atalanta's better part " was, probably, her graceful, well-proportioned
form. She was the daughter of a king of Scyros ; a great huntress, and very
swift-footed. She did not wish to marry, and, to free herself from the
importunities of her many admirers, proposed to run a race with them, the
winner to be her husband; but if she reached the goal first her competitors
were to be put to death. She would easily have distanced them all but for a
stratagem devised, we are told, by Venus, goddess of beauty.

[4] Lucretia, a Roman lady, wife of Tarquinius Collatinus, having been
dishonored by Sextus Tarquinius, revealed to her husband and father the
indignities she had suffered, entreated them to avenge her wrongs, and then
stabbed herself with a dagger she had concealed on her person.

[5] Features and traits of character.

Rosalind. O yes, I heard them all, and more too; for some of them had in them more feet than the verses would bear.

Celia. That's no matter; the feet might bear the verses.

Rosalind. Ay, but the feet were lame and could not bear themselves without the verse, and therefore stood lamely in the verse.

Celia. But didst thou hear without wondering how thy name should be hang'd and carv'd upon these trees ?

Rosalind. I was seven of the nine days out of the wonder before you came ; for look here what I found on a palm tree. I was never so berhym'd since Pythagoras'[1] time, that I was an Irish rat,[2] which I can hardly remember.

Celia. Trow you who hath done this ?

Rosalind. Is it a man ?

Celia. And a chain, that you once wore, about his neck. Change you color ?

Rosalind. I prithee, who ?

Celia. O Lord, Lord ! it is a hard matter for friends to meet; but mountains may be remov'd with earthquakes, and so encounter.

Rosalind. Nay, but who is it ?

Celia. Is it possible ?

Rosalind. Nay, I prithee now with most petitionary vehemence, tell me who it is.

Celia. O wonderful, wonderful, and most wonderful wonderful! and yet again wonderful, and after that, out of all whooping ![3]

Rosalind. Good my complexion ! dost thou think, though I am caparison'd like a man, I have a doublet and hose in my disposition ? One inch of delay more is a South Sea of discovery ; I prithee, tell me who is it quickly, and speak apace. I would

---

[1] A Greek philosopher, one of whose doctrines was the transmigration of the soul into successive bodies, either human or animal.

[2] "The belief that rats were rhymed to death in Ireland is frequently alluded to by the old dramatists."

[3] "Out of all whooping," i.e., past all exclamation.

thou couldst stammer, that thou mightst pour this conceal'd man out of thy mouth, as wine comes out of a narrow-mouth'd bottle,—either too much at once, or none at all. I prithee, take the cork out of thy mouth, that I may drink thy tidings. Is he of God's making? What manner of man? Is his head worth a hat, or his chin worth a beard?

Celia. Nay, he hath but a little beard.

Rosalind. Why, God will send more, if the man will be thankful. Let me stay [1] the growth of his beard, if thou delay me not the knowledge of his chin.

Celia. It is young Orlando, that tripp'd up the wrestler's heels and your heart both in an instant.

Rosalind. Nay, but the devil take mocking; speak, sad brow and true maid.[2]

Celia. I' faith, coz, 'tis he.

Rosalind. Orlando?

Celia. Orlando.

Rosalind. Alas the day! what shall I do with my doublet and hose?—What did he when thou saw'st him? What said he? How look'd he? Wherein went he?[3] What makes he here? Did he ask for me? Where remains he? How parted he with thee? and when shalt thou see him again? Answer me in one word.

Celia. You must borrow me Gargantua's[4] mouth first; 'tis a word too great for any mouth of this age's size. To say "ay" and "no" to these particulars is more than to answer in a catechism.

Rosalind. But doth he know that I am in this forest and in man's apparel? Looks he as freshly as he did the day he wrestled?

Celia. It is as easy to count atomies as to resolve the propositions of a lover; but take a taste of my finding him, and relish it

---

1 " Let me stay," i.e., I am willing to wait.

2 " Sad brow," etc., i.e., without joking; in honest earnest.

3 " Wherein went he?" i.e., how was he dressed?

4 A giant in one of Rabelais' satires, who swallows five pilgrims in a salad.

with good observance. I found him under a tree, like a dropp'd acorn.

Rosalind. It may well be called Jove's tree,[1] when it drops forth such fruit.

Celia. Give me audience, good madam.

Rosalind. Proceed.

Celia. There lay he, stretched along, like a wounded knight.

Rosalind. Though it be pity to see such a sight, it well becomes the ground.

Celia. Cry " holla "[2] to thy tongue, I prithee; it curvets unseasonably. He was furnish'd like a hunter.

Rosalind. O, ominous ! he comes to kill my heart.

Celia. I would sing my song without a burden; thou bring'st me out of tune.

Rosalind. Do you not know I am a woman ? when I think, I must speak. Sweet, say on.

Celia. You bring[3] me out.—Soft ! comes he not here ?

Enter ORLANDO *and* JAQUES.

Rosalind. 'Tis he ! Slink by, and note him.

Jaques. I thank you for your company; but, good faith, I had as lief have been myself alone.

Orlando. And so had I; but yet, for fashion's sake, I thank you too for your society.

Jaques. God be wi' you; let's meet as little as we can.

Orlando. I do desire we may be better strangers.

Jaques. I pray you, mar no more trees with writing love songs in their barks.

Orlando. I pray you, mar no more of my verses with reading them ill-favoredly.

Jaques. Rosalind is your love's name ?

Orlando. Yes, just.

Jaques. I do not like her name.

---

[1] The oak was sacred to Jove, or Jupiter.
[2] An expression used in checking a horse.   [3] Put.

Orlando. There was no thought of pleasing you when she was christen'd.

Jaques. What stature is she of?

Orlando. Just as high as my heart.

Jaques. You are full of pretty answers. Have you not been acquainted with goldsmiths' wives, and conn'd them out of rings?[1]

Orlando. Not so; but I answer you right painted cloth,[2] from whence you have studied your questions.

Jaques. You have a nimble wit; I think 'twas made of Atalanta's heels. Will you sit down with me? and we two will rail against our mistress the world and all our misery.

Orlando. I will chide no breather in the world but myself, against whom I know most faults.

Jaques. The worst fault you have is to be in love.

Orlando. 'Tis a fault I will not change for your best virtue. I am weary of you.

Jaques. By my troth, I was seeking for a fool when I found you.

Orlando. He is drown'd in the brook; look but in, and you shall see him.

Jaques. There I shall see mine own figure.

Orlando. Which I take to be either a fool or a cipher.

Jaques. I'll tarry no longer with you; farewell, good Signior Love.

Orlando. I am glad of your departure; adieu, good Monsieur Melancholy.　　　　　　　　　　　　　　　[*Exit Jaques.*

CELIA *and* ROSALIND *come forward.*

Rosalind. [*Aside to Celia*] I will speak to him like a saucy lackey, and under that habit play the knave with him.—Do you hear, forester?

---

[1] The meaning is, "Have you not had access to goldsmiths' shops through the favor of their wives, and studied the mottoes in rings?"

[2] "Right painted cloth," i.e., sententiously. The painted cloths often mentioned by Shakespeare were hangings of tapestry with which rooms were decorated, and on which various mottoes were wrought.

Orlando. Very well; what would you?

Rosalind. I pray you, what is't o'clock?

Orlando. You should ask me what time o' day; there's no clock in the forest.

Rosalind. Then there is no true lover in the forest; else sighing every minute and groaning every hour would detect the lazy foot of Time as well as a clock.

Orlando. And why not the swift foot of Time? Had not that been as proper?

Rosalind. By no means, sir. Time travels in divers paces with divers persons. I'll tell you who Time ambles withal, who Time trots withal, who Time gallops withal, and who he stands still withal.

Orlando. I prithee, who doth he trot withal?

Rosalind. Marry, he trots hard with a young maid between the contract of her marriage and the day it is solemniz'd. If the interim be but a se'nnight,[1] Time's pace is so hard that it seems the length of seven year.

Orlando. Who ambles Time withal?

Rosalind. With a priest that lacks Latin and a rich man that hath not the gout; for the one sleeps easily because he cannot study, and the other lives merrily because he feels no pain,—the one lacking the burden of lean and wasteful learning, the other knowing no burden of heavy, tedious penury. These Time ambles withal.

Orlando. Who doth he gallop withal?

Rosalind. With a thief to the gallows; for though he go as softly as foot can fall, he thinks himself too soon there.

Orlando. Who stays he still withal?

Rosalind. With lawyers in the vacation; for they sleep between term and term, and then they perceive not how Time moves.

Orlando. Where dwell you, pretty youth?

---

1 Seven nights, i.e., a week; as we say "fortnight," i.e., fourteen nights, for two weeks.

Rosalind. With this shepherdess, my sister, here in the skirts of the forest, like fringe upon a petticoat.

Orlando. Are you native of this place?

Rosalind. As the cony that you see dwell where she is kindled.[1]

Orlando. Your accent is something finer than you could purchase[2] in so remov'd a dwelling.

Rosalind. I have been told so of many; but, indeed, an old religious uncle of mine taught me to speak, who was in his youth an inland man; one that knew courtship[3] too well, for there he fell in love. I have heard him read many lectures against it, and I thank God I am not a woman, to be touch'd with so many giddy offenses as he hath generally tax'd their whole sex withal.

Orlando. Can you remember any of the principal evils that he laid to the charge of women?

Rosalind. There were none principal; they were all like one another as half-pence are, every one fault seeming monstrous till his fellow-fault came to match it.

Orlando. I prithee, recount some of them.

Rosalind. No, I will not cast away my physic but on those that are sick. There is a man haunts the forest, that abuses our young plants with carving "Rosalind" on their barks; hangs odes upon hawthorns and elegies on brambles, all, forsooth, deifying the name of Rosalind. If I could meet that fancymonger,[4] I would give him some good counsel, for he seems to have the quotidian[5] of love upon him.

Orlando. I am he that is so love-shak'd; I pray you, tell me your remedy.

Rosalind. There is none of my uncle's marks upon you. He taught me how to know a man in love, in which cage of rushes I am sure you are not prisoner.

Orlando. What were his marks?

---

[1] Brought forth.   [2] Acquire.
[3] Court manners.   Rosalind puns on the word.   [4] One who deals in love.
[5] Quotidian fevers are those in which the paroxysms occur daily.

Rosalind. A lean cheek, which you have not; a blue eye,[1] and sunken, which you have not; an unquestionable[2] spirit, which you have not; a beard neglected, which you have not — but I pardon you for that, for simply[3] your having[4] in beard is a younger brother's revenue; then your hose should be ungarter'd, your bonnet unbanded, your sleeve unbutton'd, your shoe unti'd, and everything about you demonstrating a careless desolation. But you are no such man; you are rather point-device[5] in your accouterments, as loving yourself, than seeming the lover of any other.

Orlando. Fair youth, I would I could make thee believe I love.

Rosalind. Me[6] believe it ! You may as soon make her that you love believe it, which, I warrant, she is apter to do than to confess she does; that is one of the points in the which women still give the lie to their consciences. But, in good sooth, are you he that hangs the verses on the trees, wherein Rosalind is so admired ?

Orlando. I swear to thee, youth, by the white hand of Rosalind, I am that he, that unfortunate he.

Rosalind. But are you so much in love as your rhymes speak ?

Orlando. Neither rhyme nor reason can express how much.

Rosalind. Love is merely a madness, and, I tell you, deserves as well a dark house and a whip[7] as madmen do; and the reason why they are not so punished and cured is that the lunacy is so ordinary that the whippers are in love too. Yet I profess curing it by counsel.

Orlando. Did you ever cure any so ?

Rosalind. Yes, one, and in this manner. He was to imagine me his love, his mistress, and I set him every day to woo me; at which time would I, being but a moonish[8] youth, grieve, be

---

[1] " Blue eye," i.e., blue beneath the eyelids, not in the iris.
[2] Unsociable.   [3] Indeed.   [4] Property.   [5] Faultless.
[6] Object of " make " understood.
[7] This barbarous treatment of lunatics prevailed till within the last fifty years.   [8] Changeable.

effeminate, changeable, longing and liking, proud, fantastical, apish, shallow, inconstant, full of tears, full of smiles, for every passion something and for no passion truly anything, as boys and women are for the most part cattle of this color; would now like him, now loathe him; then entertain him, then forswear him; now weep for him, then spit at him; that I drave my suitor from his mad humor of love to a living[1] humor of madness; which was, to forswear the full stream of the world and to live in a nook merely[2] monastic. And thus I cured him; and this way will I take upon me to wash your liver[3] as clean as a sound sheep's heart, that there shall not be one spot of love in't.

Orlando. I would not be cured, youth.

Rosalind. I would cure you, if you would but call me Rosalind and come every day to my cote and woo me.

Orlando. Now, by the faith of my love, I will; tell me where it is.

Rosalind. Go with me to it and I'll show it you; and by the way you shall tell me where in the forest you live. Will you go?

Orlando. With all my heart, good youth.

Rosalind. Nay, you must call me Rosalind.—Come, sister, will you go?   [*Exeunt.*

Scene III. *The Forest.*

Enter Touchstone *and* Audrey; Jaques *behind.*

Touchstone. Come apace,[4] good Audrey; I will fetch up your goats, Audrey. And how, Audrey? am I the man yet? Doth my simple feature[5] content you?

Audrey. Your features! Lord warrant us! what features?

Touchstone. I am here with thee and thy goats, as the most capricious poet, honest Ovid, was among the Goths.[6]

---

[1] Real.   [2] Entirely.

[3] Old physiologists regarded the liver as the seat of the affections.

[4] Quickly.   [5] Personal appearance.

[6] A pun is intended on the words "goats" and "Goths," the old pronunciation of Goths being as though it were spelled "Gotes." The pun is

Jaques. [*Aside*] O knowledge ill inhabited, worse than Jove in a thatch'd house !¹

Touchstone. When a man's verses cannot be understood, nor a man's good wit seconded with the forward child Understanding, it strikes a man more dead than a great reckoning in a little room.² Truly, I would the gods had made thee poetical.

Audrey. I do not know what "poetical" is. Is it honest in deed and word ? Is it a true thing ?

Touchstone. No, truly; for the truest poetry is the most feigning; and lovers are given to poetry, and what they swear in poetry may be said as lovers they do feign.

Audrey. Do you wish, then, that the gods had made me poetical ?

Touchstone. I do, truly; for thou swear'st to me thou art honest; now, if thou wert a poet, I might have some hope thou didst feign.

Audrey. Would you not have me honest ?

Touchstone. No, truly, unless thou wert hard-favored; for honesty coupled to beauty is to have honey a sauce to sugar.

Jaques. [*Aside*] A material³ fool !

Audrey. Well, I am not fair; and therefore I pray the gods make me honest.

Touchstone. Truly, and to cast away honesty upon a foul⁴ slut were to put good meat into an unclean dish.

Audrey. I am not a slut, though I thank the gods I am foul.

Touchstone. Well, praised be the gods for thy foulness ! sluttishness may come hereafter. But be it as it may be, I will

---

helped out by the word "capricious," which is derived from the Latin *caper* ("goat").

¹ Jupiter and Mercury, visiting the earth in disguise, came upon the humble dwelling of Philemon and Baucis, and were so hospitably entertained by the worthy couple that Jupiter changed their thatched cottage into a superb temple, of which Baucis and her husband were made priests. (See GUERBER'S *Myths of Greece and Rome*, p. 43.)

² "Great reckoning," etc., i.e., a large bill for a small accommodation.

³ Full of matter; sensible.   ⁴ Homely.

marry thee; and to that end I have been with Sir Oliver Martext, the vicar of the next village, who hath promis'd to meet me
in this place of the forest and to couple us.

Jaques. [*Aside*] I would fain see this meeting.

Audrey. Well, the gods give us joy!

Touchstone. Amen! Here comes Sir Oliver.—

Enter SIR OLIVER MARTEXT.

Sir Oliver Martext, you are well met. Will you dispatch us here
under this tree, or shall we go with you to your chapel?

Sir Oliver. Is there none here to give the woman?

Touchstone. I will not take her on gift of any man.

Sir Oliver. Truly, she must be given, or the marriage is not
lawful.

Jaques. [*Advancing*] Proceed, proceed; I'll give her.

Touchstone. Good even, good Master What-ye-call't; how do
you, sir? You are very well met. God 'ild [1] you for your last
company; I am very glad to see you;—even a toy [2] in hand
here, sir;—nay, pray be cover'd.

Jaques. Will you be married, motley?

Touchstone. As the ox hath his bow,[3] sir, the horse his curb,
and the falcon her bells, so man hath his desires; and as pigeons
bill, so wedlock would be nibbling.

Jaques. And will you, being a man of your breeding, be married under a bush like a beggar? Get you to church, and have
a good priest that can tell you what marriage is. This fellow will
but join you together as they join wainscot; then one of you will
prove a shrunk panel, and, like green timber, warp, warp.

Touchstone. [*Aside*] I am not in the mind but I were better to
be married of him than of another; for he is not like to marry
me well, and not being well married, it will be a good excuse
for me hereafter to leave my wife.

Jaques. Go thou with me, and let me counsel thee.

1 Yield; reward.   2 A trifling matter.   3 Yoke.

Touchstone. Come, sweet Audrey. —
Farewell, good Master Oliver; not, —

> *O sweet Oliver,*
> *O brave Oliver,*
> *Leave me not behind thee:*

but, —

> *Wind away,*
> *Begone, I say,*
> *I will not to wedding with thee.*
>
> [*Exeunt Jaques, Touchstone, and Audrey.*

Sir Oliver. 'Tis no matter; ne'er a fantastical knave of them all shall flout me out of my calling.   [*Exit.*

SCENE IV. *The Forest.*

Enter ROSALIND *and* CELIA.

Rosalind. Never talk to me; I will weep.

Celia. Do, I prithee; but yet have the grace to consider that tears do not become a man.

Rosalind. But have I not cause to weep?

Celia. As good cause as one would desire; therefore weep.

Rosalind. His very hair is of the dissembling color.

Celia. Something browner than Judas's; [1] marry, his kisses are Judas's own children.

Rosalind. I' faith, his hair is of a good color.

Celia. An excellent color; your chestnut was ever the only color.

Rosalind. And his kissing is as full of sanctity as the touch of holy bread.

Celia. He hath bought a pair of chaste lips of Diana.[2] A nun of winter's sisterhood kisses not more religiously; the very ice of chastity is in them.

---

[1] Judas is constantly represented in old paintings and tapestries with red hair and beard.

[2] See Note 5, p. 53.

Rosalind. But why did he swear he would come this morning, and comes not?

Celia. Nay, certainly, there is no truth in him.

Rosalind. Do you think so?

Celia. Yes; I think he is not a pickpurse nor a horse stealer, but for his verity in love, I do think him as concave as a covered goblet or a worm-eaten nut.

Rosalind. Not true in love?

Celia. Yes, when he is in; but I think he is not in.

Rosalind. You have heard him swear downright he was.

Celia. "Was" is not "is;" besides, the oath of a lover is no stronger than the word of a tapster; they are both the confirmers of false reckonings. He attends here in the forest on the Duke your father.

Rosalind. I met the Duke yesterday, and had much question with him. He ask'd me of what parentage I was; I told him, of as good as he; so he laugh'd and let me go. But what talk we of fathers, when there is such a man as Orlando?

Celia. O, that's a brave man! He writes brave verses, speaks brave words, swears brave oaths and breaks them bravely, quite traverse, athwart the heart of his lover; as a puisny [1] tilter, that spurs his horse but on one side, breaks his staff like a noble goose. But all's brave that youth mounts and folly guides.—Who comes here?

Enter CORIN.

Corin. Mistress and master, you have oft inquired
After the shepherd that complain'd of love,
Whom you saw sitting by me on the turf,
Praising the proud, disdainful shepherdess
That was his mistress.

Celia.   Well, and what of him?

Corin. If you will see a pageant truly play'd,
Between the pale complexion of true love

---

[1] Unskillful.

And the red glow of scorn and proud disdain,
Go hence a little and I shall conduct you,
If you will mark it.
 Rosalind.   O, come, let us remove;
The sight of lovers feedeth those in love. —
Bring us to see this sight, and you shall say
I'll prove a busy actor in their play.   [*Exeunt.*

SCENE V. *Another Part of the Forest.*

Enter SILVIUS *and* PHEBE.

Silvius. Sweet Phebe, do not scorn me; do not, Phebe;
Say that you love me not, but say not so
In bitterness. The common executioner,
Whose heart the accustom'd sight of death makes hard,
Falls not the ax ¹ upon the humbled neck
But first begs pardon. Will you sterner be
Than he that dies and lives ² by bloody drops ?

Enter ROSALIND, CELIA, *and* CORIN, *behind.*

Phebe. I would not be thy executioner;
I fly thee, for I would not injure thee.
Thou tell'st me there is murder in mine eye !
'Tis pretty, sure, and very probable,
That eyes, that are the frail'st and softest things,
Who shut their coward gates on atomies,
Should be call'd tyrants, butchers, murderers !
Now I do frown on thee with all my heart;
And if mine eyes can wound, now let them kill thee!
Now counterfeit to swoon; why, now fall down;
Or if thou canst not, O, for shame, for shame!
Lie not, to say mine eyes are murderers !
Now show the wound mine eye hath made in thee.

---

¹ " Falls not the ax," i.e., lets not the ax fall.
² " Dies and lives," i.e., lives and dies ; earns a livelihood.

Scratch thee but with a pin, and there remains
Some scar of it; lean but upon a rush,
The cicatrice [1] and capable impressure [2]
Thy palm some moment keeps; but now mine eyes,
Which I have darted at hee, hurt thee not;
Nor, I am sure, there is no force in eyes
That can do hurt.

    Silvius.   O dear Phebe,
If ever—as that ever may be near—
You meet in some fresh cheek the power of fancy,
Then shall you know the wounds invisible
That love's keen arrows make.

    Phebe.   But till that time
Come not thou near me; and when that time comes,
Afflict me with thy mocks, pity me not;
As till that time I shall not pity thee.

    Rosalind. [*Advancing*] And why, I pray you? Who might
        be your mother,
That you insult, exult, and all at once,
Over the wretched? What though you have no beauty,—
As, by my faith, I see no more in you
Than without candle may go dark to bed,—
Must you be therefore proud and pitiless?
Why, what means this? Why do you look on me?
I see no more in you than in the ordinary
Of Nature's salework.—'Od's my little life,
I think she means to tangle my eyes too!—
No, faith, proud mistress, hope not after it.
'Tis not your inky brows, your black-silk hair,
Your bugle [3] eyeballs, nor your cheek of cream,
That can entame my spirits to your worship.—
You foolish shepherd, wherefore do you follow her,
Like foggy south puffing with wind and rain?

---

[1] Scar; mark.   [2] " Capable impressure," i.e., sensible impression.
[3] Jet black, like the beads called " bugles."

You are a thousand times a properer [1] man
Than she a woman.   'Tis such fools as you
That make the world full of ill-favor'd children.
'Tis not her glass, but you, that flatters her;
And out of you she sees herself more proper
Than any of her lineaments can show her.—
But, mistress, know yourself; down on your knees,
And thank Heaven, fasting, for a good man's love;
For I must tell you friendly in your ear,
Sell when you can,—you are not for all markets.
Cry the man mercy; love him; take his offer.
Foul is most foul, being foul to be a scoffer.—
So take her to thee, shepherd; fare you well.

Phebe.   Sweet youth, I pray you, chide a year together;
I had rather hear you chide than this man woo.

Rosalind.   He's fallen in love with your foulness,[2]—and she'll
fall in love with my anger.   If it be so, as fast as she answers thee
with frowning looks, I'll sauce her with bitter words.—Why look
you so upon me?

Phebe.   For no ill will I bear you.

Rosalind.   I pray you, do not fall in love with me,
For I am falser than vows made in wine;
Besides, I like you not.—If you will know my house,
'Tis at the tuft of olives here hard by.—
Will you go, sister?—Shepherd, ply her hard.—
Come, sister.—Shepherdess, look on him better,
And be not proud; though all the world could see,
None could be so abus'd [3] in sight as he.—
Come, to our flock.   [*Exeunt Rosalind, Celia, and Corin.*

Phebe.   Dead shepherd,[4] now I find thy saw of might:
" Who ever loved that loved not at first sight?"

---

[1] Handsomer.   [2] See Note 4, p. 67.   [3] Deceived.
[4] The reference is to Christopher Marlowe, who died in 1593; and the
line quoted is from his Hero and Leander.   " ' Shepherd ' is used for ' poet '
in the language of pastoral poetry."

Silvius. Sweet Phebe,—

Phebe.   Ha, what say'st thou, Silvius ?

Silvius. Sweet Phebe, pity me.

Phebe. Why, I am sorry for thee, gentle Silvius.

Silvius. Wherever sorrow is, relief would be ;
If you do sorrow at my grief in love,
By giving love your sorrow and my grief
Were both extermin'd.[1]

Phebe. Thou hast my love; is not that neighborly ?

Silvius. I would have you.

Phebe.   Why, that were covetousness.
Silvius, the time was that I hated thee,
And yet it is not that I bear thee love ;
But since that thou canst talk of love so well,
Thy company, which erst [2] was irksome to me,
I will endure ; and I'll employ thee too ;
But do not look for further recompense
Than thine own gladness that thou art employ'd.

    Silvius. So holy and so perfect is my love,
And I in such a poverty of grace,
That I shall think it a most plenteous crop
To glean the broken ears after the man
That the main harvest reaps.   Loose now and then
A scatter'd smile, and that I'll live upon.

    Phebe. Know'st thou the youth that spoke to me erewhile ?

    Silvius. Not very well, but I have met him oft ;
And he hath bought the cottage and the bounds
That the old carlot [3] once was master of.

    Phebe. Think not I love him, though I ask for him ;
'Tis but a peevish [4] boy ;—yet he talks well.
But what care I for words ? yet words do well
When he that speaks them pleases those that hear.
It is a pretty youth—not very pretty ;
But, sure, he's proud, and yet his pride becomes him ;

---

    [1] Exterminated.   [2] Lately.   [3] Rustic.   [4] Wayward.

He'll make a proper man.   The best thing in him
Is his complexion ; and faster than his tongue
Did make offense his eye did heal it up.
He is not very tall, yet for his years he's tall ;
His leg is but so-so, and yet 'tis well ;
There was a pretty redness in his lip,
A little riper and more lusty red
Than that mix'd in his cheek ; 'twas just the difference
Betwixt the constant [1] red and mingled damask.
There be some women, Silvius, had they mark'd him
In parcels [2] as I did, would have gone near
To fall in love with him ; but, for my part,
I love him not nor hate him not ; and yet
I have more cause to hate him than to love him ;
For what had he to do to chide at me ?
He said mine eyes were black and my hair black ;
And, now I am remember'd, scorn'd at me.
I marvel why I answer'd not again ;
But that's all one — omittance is no quittance.
I'll write to him a very taunting letter,
And thou shalt bear it ; wilt thou, Silvius ?
 Silvius.   Phebe, with all my heart.
 Phebe.   I'll write it straight ;
The matter's in my head and in my heart ;
I will be bitter with him, and passing short.
Go with me, Silvius.   [*Exeunt.*

ACT IV.

SCENE I. *The Forest.*

Enter ROSALIND, CELIA, *and* JAQUES.

Jaques. I prithee, pretty youth, let me be better acquainted
with thee.

 Rosalind. They say you are a melancholy fellow.

---

1 Uniform.   2 Detail.

Jaques. I am so; I do love it better than laughing.

Rosalind. Those that are in extremity of either are abominable fellows, and betray themselves to every modern censure [1] worse than drunkards.

Jaques. Why, 'tis good to be sad and say nothing.

Rosalind. Why, then, 'tis good to be a post.

Jaques. I have neither the scholar's melancholy, which is emulation, nor the musician's, which is fantastical, nor the courtier's, which is proud, nor the soldier's, which is ambitious, nor the lawyer's, which is politic, nor the lady's, which is nice,[2] nor the lover's, which is all these; but it is a melancholy of mine own, compounded of many simples, extracted from many objects, and, indeed, the sundry contemplation of my travels, in which my often rumination wraps me in a most humorous [3] sadness.

Rosalind. A traveler! By my faith, you have great reason to be sad. I fear you have sold your own lands to see other men's; then to have seen much and to have nothing is to have rich eyes and poor hands.

Jaques. Yes, I have gain'd my experience.

Rosalind. And your experience makes you sad. I had rather have a fool to make me merry than experience to make me sad; and to travel for it too!

Enter ORLANDO.

Orlando. Good day and happiness, dear Rosalind!

Jaques. Nay, then, God be wi' you, an[4] you talk in blank verse.   [*Exit.*

Rosalind. Farewell, Monsieur Traveler; look you lisp and wear strange suits, disable [5] all the benefits of your own country, be out of love with your nativity, and almost chide God for making you that countenance you are, or I will scarce think you have swam in a gondola.[6]—Why, how now, Orlando! where have

---

[1] "Modern censure," i.e., ordinary judgment.
[2] Fastidious.   [3] Fanciful.   [4] If.   [5] Depreciate.
[6] Venice, built on small islands in a lagoon, is intersected by canals; and

you been all this while ?   You a lover !   An you serve me such another trick, never come in my sight more.

Orlando. My fair Rosalind, I come within an hour of my promise.

Rosalind. Break an hour's promise in love !   He that will divide a minute into a thousand parts, and break but a part of the thousandth part of a minute in the affairs of love, it may be said of him that Cupid hath clapped him o' the shoulder, but I'll warrant him heart-whole.

Orlando. Pardon me, dear Rosalind.

Rosalind. Nay, an you be so tardy, come no more in my sight.   I had as lief be woo'd of a snail.

Orlando. Of a snail ?

Rosalind. Ay, of a snail ; for though he comes slowly, he carries his house on his head,—a better jointure,[1] I think, than you can make a woman.   Come, woo me, woo me, for now I am in a holiday humor and like enough to consent.   What would you say to me now, an I were your very, very Rosalind ?

Orlando. I would kiss before I spoke.

Rosalind. Nay, you were better speak first, and when you were graveled[2] for lack of matter, you might take occasion to kiss.   Very good orators, when they are out, they will spit ; and for lovers lacking — God warn us! — matter, the cleanliest shift is to kiss.

Orlando. How if the kiss be denied ?

Rosalind. Then she puts you to entreaty, and there begins new matter.

Orlando. Who could be out, being before his beloved mistress ?

the gondola, the Venetian pleasure boat, serves the purpose of the cab or omnibus of other cities.   In the sixteenth century Venice, being one of the gayest and most attractive capitals of Europe, was a great resort of travelers ; and one who had never visited that city — never " swam in a gondola " — was hardly counted a traveler at all.

1 " The settlement of property made at marriage on the wife, in case of her husband dying before her."

2 Run aground, figuratively.

Rosalind. Marry, that should you, if I were your mistress, or I should think my honesty ranker than my wit.

Orlando. What, of my suit ?

Rosalind. Not out of your apparel, and yet out of your suit. Am not I your Rosalind ?

Orlando. I take some joy to say you are, because I would be talking of her.

Rosalind. Well, in her person I say I will not have you.

Orlando. Then in mine own person I die.

Rosalind. No, faith, die by attorney.[1] The poor world is almost six thousand years old, and in all this time there was not any man died in his own person, videlicet,[2] in a love cause. Troilus[3] had his brains dash'd out with a Grecian club; yet he did what he could to die before, and he is one of the patterns of love. Leander, he would have liv'd many a fair year, though Hero had turn'd nun, if it had not been for a hot midsummer night; for, good youth, he went but forth to wash him in the Hellespont, and being taken with the cramp, was drown'd; and the foolish chroniclers of that age found it was " Hero of Sestos."[4] But these are all lies; men have died from time to time, and worms have eaten them, but not for love.

Orlando. I would not have my right Rosalind of this mind, for, I protest, her frown might kill me.

Rosalind. By this hand, it will not kill a fly. But come, now

---

[1] Substitute.

[2] Namely; usually abbreviated to *viz.*

[3] A son of Priam, King of Troy, who was killed by Achilles during the Trojan War. The story of his love for Cressida, his faith and her perfidy, is the subject of Shakespeare's tragedy of Troilus and Cressida.

[4] " Leander . . . Hero of Sestos." The story, the theme of many poets, is familiar. Leander, a youth of Abydos, enamored of Hero, a priestess of Venus at Sestos, nightly swam the Hellespont to meet her, she guiding his course by a torchlight displayed from a high tower; till on one wild and stormy night the adventurous lover was drowned, and Hero in despair threw herself into the sea and perished in the waves. (See GUERBER'S *Myths of Greece and Rome*, pp. 111–117.)

I will be your Rosalind in a more coming-on disposition, and ask me what you will, I will grant it.

Orlando. Then love me, Rosalind.

Rosalind. Yes, faith, will I, Fridays and Saturdays and all.

Orlando. And wilt thou have me ?

Rosalind. Ay, and twenty such.

Orlando. What sayest thou ?

Rosalind. Are you not good ?

Orlando. I hope so.

Rosalind. Why, then, can one desire too much of a good thing ? — Come, sister, you shall be the priest and marry us. — Give me your hand, Orlando. — What do you say, sister ?

Orlando. Pray thee, marry us.

Celia. I cannot say the words.

Rosalind. You must begin, " Will you, Orlando,"—

Celia. Go to. — Will you, Orlando, have to wife this Rosalind ?

Orlando. I will.

Rosalind. Ay, but when ?

Orlando. Why, now ; as fast as she can marry us.

Rosalind. Then you must say, " I take thee, Rosalind, for wife."

Orlando. I take thee, Rosalind, for wife.

Rosalind. I might ask you for your commission ; [1] but — I do take thee, Orlando, for my husband. There's a girl goes before the priest ; and certainly a woman's thought runs before her actions.

Orlando. So do all thoughts ; they are wing'd.

Rosalind. Now tell me how long you would have her after you have possess'd her.

Orlando. For ever and a day.

Rosalind. Say "a day," without the "ever." No, no, Orlando ; men are April when they woo, December when they wed ; maids are May when they are maids, but the sky changes when they are wives. I will be more jealous of thee than a Barbary cock pigeon over his hen, more clamorous than a parrot against rain,

---

[1] Warrant ; authority.

more newfangled[1] than an ape, more giddy in my desires than a
monkey; I will weep for nothing, like Diana in the fountain,[2]
and I will do that when you are dispos'd to be merry; I will
laugh like a hyen,[3] and that when thou art inclin'd to sleep.

Orlando. But will my Rosalind do so ?

Rosalind. By my life, she will do as I do.

Orlando. O, but she is wise.

Rosalind. Or else she could not have the wit to do this; the
wiser, the waywarder. Make[4] the doors upon a woman's wit,
and it will out at the casement; shut that, and 'twill out at the
keyhole; stop that, 'twill fly with the smoke out at the chimney.

Orlando. For these two hours, Rosalind, I will leave thee.

Rosalind. Alas ! dear love, I cannot lack thee two hours.

Orlando. I must attend the Duke at dinner; by two o'clock I
will be with thee again.

Rosalind. Ay, go your ways, go your ways; I knew what you
would prove. My friends told me as much, and I thought no
less. That flattering tongue of yours won me; 'tis but one cast
away, and so, come, death ! — Two o'clock is your hour ?

Orlando. Ay, sweet Rosalind.

Rosalind. By my troth, and in good earnest, and so God mend
me, and by all pretty oaths that are not dangerous, if you break
one jot of your promise, or come one minute behind your hour, I
will think you the most pathetical[5] break-promise, and the most
hollow lover, and the most unworthy of her you call Rosalind,
that may be chosen out of the gross band of the unfaithful;
therefore beware my censure and keep your promise.

Orlando. With no less religion than if thou wert indeed my
Rosalind. So, adieu !

Rosalind. Well, Time is the old justice that examines all such
offenders, and let Time try. Adieu.   [*Exit Orlando.*

---

[1] Changeable.

[2] Images of Diana were, and are, frequent ornaments in fountains.

[3] Hyena. The bark of this animal is not unlike a rude laugh.

[4] Close.   [5] Canting; used here in a ludicrous sense.

Celia. You have simply misused our sex in your love prate.

Rosalind. O coz, coz, coz, my pretty little coz, that thou didst know how many fathom deep I am in love ! But it cannot be sounded ; my affection hath an unknown bottom, like the bay of Portugal. [1]

Celia. Or rather, bottomless, that as fast as you pour affection in, it runs out.

Rosalind. No, that same wicked bastard of Venus that was begot of thought, conceived of spleen, and born of madness, — that blind, rascally boy that abuses every one's eyes because his own are out, — let him be judge how deep I am in love. I'll tell thee, Aliena, I cannot be out of the sight of Orlando; I'll go find a shadow,[2] and sigh till he come.

Celia. And I'll sleep.   [*Exeunt.*

SCENE II. *The Forest.*

Enter JAQUES, Lords, *and* Foresters.

Jaques. Which is he that killed the deer ?

A Lord. Sir, it was I.

Jaques. Let's present him to the Duke, like a Roman conqueror; and it would do well to set the deer's horns upon his head, for a branch of victory. — Have you no song, forester, for this purpose ?

Forester. Yes, sir.

Jaques. Sing it; 'tis no matter how it be in tune, so it make noise enough.

SONG.

Forester.   *What shall he have that kill'd the deer?*
　　　　　His leather skin and horns to wear.
　　　　　　Then sing him home ;
　　　　　　　　[The rest shall bear this burden.

---

[1] There is no such bay recognized by geographers; but off the coast of Portugal, near Oporto, the water is exceedingly deep, and at a distance of twenty miles from shore attains a depth of eighty-five hundred feet.

[2] Shady place.

Take thou no scorn to wear the horn ;
It was a crest ere thou wast born :
Thy father's father wore it,
And thy father bore it
The horn, the horn, the lusty horn,
Is not a thing to laugh to scorn.   [*Exeunt.*

SCENE III. *The Forest.*

Enter ROSALIND *and* CELIA.

Rosalind. How say you now ?   Is it not past two o'clock ?
and here much Orlando !

Celia. I warrant you, with pure love and troubled brain, he
hath ta'en his bow and arrows and is gone forth—to sleep.—
Look who comes here.

Enter SILVIUS.

Silvius. My errand is to you, fair youth.
My gentle Phebe bid me give you this.   [*Giving a letter.*
I know not the contents'; but, as I guess
By the stern brow and waspish action
Which she did use as she was writing of it,
It bears an angry tenor.   Pardon me;
I am but as a guiltless messenger.

Rosalind. Patience herself would startle at this letter,
And play the swaggerer; bear this, bear all!
She says I am not fair, that I lack manners;
She calls me proud, and that she could not love me
Were man as rare as phenix.[1]   'Od's my will !
Her love is not the hare that I do hunt.
Why writes she so to me ? — Well, shepherd, well,
This is a letter of your own device.

---

[1] According to the old and familiar fable, this bird, after living five hundred years, destroys itself by fire, and its successor arises from the ashes,
there being but one phenix in existence at a time.

Silvius. No, I protest, I know not the contents';
Phebe did write it.

Rosalind.   Come, come, you are a fool,
And turn'd into the extremity of love.
I saw her hand; she has a leathern hand,
A freestone-color'd hand; I verily did think
That her old gloves were on, but 'twas her hands;
She has a huswife's hand; but that's no matter.
I say she never did invent this letter;
This is a man's invention and his hand.

Silvius. Sure, it is hers.

Rosalind. Why, 'tis a boisterous and a cruel style,
A style for challengers; why, she defies me,
Like Turk to Christian!   Woman's gentle brain
Could not drop forth such giant-rude invention,
Such Ethiop words, blacker in their effect
Than in their countenance.   Will you hear the letter?

Silvius. So please you, for I never heard it yet;
Yet heard too much of Phebe's cruelty.

Rosalind. She Phebes me; mark how the tyrant writes.

                                        [*Reads.*

         Art thou god to shepherd turn'd,
         That a maiden's heart hath burn'd?—

Can a woman rail thus?—
  Silvius. Call you this railing?
  Rosalind. [*Reads*]

         Why, thy godhead laid apart,
         Warr'st thou with a woman's heart?—

Did you ever hear such railing?—

         Whiles the eye of man did woo me,
         That could do no vengeance to me.—

Meaning me a beast.—

If the scorn of your bright eyne [1]
Have power to raise such love in mine,
Alack, in me what strange effect
Would they work in mild aspect' !
Whiles you chid me, I did love ;
How then might your prayers move !
He that brings this love to thee
Little knows this love in me ;
And by him seal up thy mind ;
Whether that thy youth and kind [2]
Will the faithful offer take
Of me and all that I can make ;
Or else by him my love deny,
And then I'll study how to die.

Silvius. Call you this chiding ?

Celia. Alas, poor shepherd !

Rosalind. Do you pity him ? No, he deserves no pity. — Wilt thou love such a woman ? What, to make thee an instrument and play false strains upon thee ! — not to be endur'd ! — Well, go your way to her — for I see love hath made thee a tame snake [3] — and say this to her: that if she love me, I charge her to love thee; if she will not, I will never have her unless thou entreat for her. If you be a true lover, hence, and not a word; for here comes more company.   [*Exit Silvius.*

Enter OLIVER.

Oliver. Good morrow, fair ones; pray you, if you know,
Where in the purlieus [4] of this forest stands
A sheepcote fenc'd about with olive trees ?

Celia. West of this place, down in the neighbor bottom;
The rank [5] of osiers by the murmuring stream
Left on your right hand brings you to the place.
But at this hour the house doth keep itself;
There's none within.

---

1 The old plural of "eye."   2 Natural disposition.
3 Contemptible fellow.   4 Borders.   5 Row.

Oliver. If that an eye may profit by a tongue,
Then should I know you by description;
Such garments and such years: "The boy is fair,
Of female favor, and bestows [1] himself
Like a ripe [2] sister; the woman low,
And browner than her brother." Are not you
The owner of the house I did inquire for?
　　Celia. It is no boast, being ask'd, to say we are.
　　Oliver. Orlando doth commend him to you both,
And to that youth he calls his Rosalind
He sends this bloody napkin.[3]—Are you he?
　　Rosalind. I am. What must we understand by this?
　　Oliver. Some of my shame; if you will know of me
What man I am, and how and why and where
This handkercher was stain'd.
　　Celia.　　　　　　　　I pray you, tell it.
　　Oliver. When last the young Orlando parted from you
He left a promise to return again
Within an hour; and pacing through the forest,
Chewing the food of sweet and bitter fancy,
Lo, what befell! He threw his eye aside,
And mark what object did present itself;
Under an oak, whose boughs were moss'd with age,
And high top bald with dry antiquity,
A wretched, ragged man, o'ergrown with hair,
Lay sleeping on his back. About his neck
A green and gilded snake had wreath'd itself,
Who with her head, nimble in threats, approach'd
The opening of his mouth; but suddenly,
Seeing Orlando, it unlink'd itself,
And with indented glides did slip away
Into a bush; under which bush's shade
A lioness, with udders all drawn dry,
Lay couching,[4] head on ground, with catlike watch,

---

[1] Conducts.　　　[2] Elder.　　　[3] Handkerchief.　　　[4] Crouching.

When that the sleeping man should stir; for 'tis
The royal disposition of that beast
To prey on nothing that doth seem as dead.
This seen, Orlando did approach the man,
And found it was his brother, his elder brother.

 Celia. O, I have heard him speak of that same brother;
And he did render [1] him the most unnatural
That liv'd 'mongst men.

 Oliver.   And well he might so do,
For well I know he was unnatural.

 Rosalind. But, to Orlando: did he leave him there,
Food to the suck'd and hungry lioness?

 Oliver. Twice did he turn his back and purpos'd so;
But kindness, nobler ever than revenge,
And nature, stronger than his just occasion,
Made him give battle to the lioness,
Who quickly fell before him; in which hurtling [2]
From miserable slumber I awaked.

 Celia. Are you his brother?

 Rosalind.   Was't you he rescu'd?

 Celia. Was't you that did so oft contrive to kill him?

 Oliver. 'Twas I; but 'tis not I. I do not shame
To tell you what I was, since my conversion
So sweetly tastes, being the thing I am.

 Rosalind. But, for the bloody napkin?

 Oliver.   By and by.
When from the first to last betwixt us two
Tears our recountments had most kindly bath'd,
As how I came into that desert place;—
In brief, he led me to the gentle Duke,
Who gave me fresh array and entertainment,
Committing me unto my brother's love;
Who led me instantly unto his cave,
There stripp'd himself, and here upon his arm

   [1] Report.   [2] Noise of the conflict.

The lioness had torn some flesh away,
Which all this while had bled ; and now he fainted,
And cried, in fainting, upon Rosalind.
Brief, I recover'd him, bound up his wound ;
And, after some small space, being strong at heart,
He sent me hither, stranger as I am,
To tell this story, that you might excuse
His broken promise, and to give this napkin
Dyed in his blood unto the shepherd youth
That he in sport doth call his Rosalind.   [*Rosalind swoons.*

Celia. Why, how now, Ganymede ! sweet Ganymede !

Oliver. Many will swoon when they do look on blood.

Celia. There is more in it. — Cousin — Ganymede !

Oliver. Look, he recovers.

Rosalind. I would I were at home.

Celia.   We'll lead you thither. —
I pray you, will you take him by the arm ?

Oliver. Be of good cheer, youth. You a man! you lack a
man's heart.

Rosalind. I do so, I confess it. Ah, sirrah, a body would
think this was well counterfeited ! I pray you, tell your brother
how well I counterfeited. — Heigh-ho !

Oliver. This was not counterfeit ; there is too great testimony
in your complexion that it was a passion of earnest.

Rosalind. Counterfeit, I assure you.

Oliver. Well, then, take a good heart and counterfeit to be a
man.

Rosalind. So I do ; but, i' faith, I should have been a woman
by right.

Celia. Come, you look paler and paler; pray you, draw
homewards. — Good sir, go with us.

Oliver. That will I, for I must bear answer back
How you excuse my brother, Rosalind.

Rosalind. I shall devise something ; but, I pray you, commend my counterfeiting to him. — Will you go ?   [*Exeunt.*

ACT V.

SCENE I. *The Forest.*

Enter TOUCHSTONE *and* AUDREY.

Touchstone. We shall find a time, Audrey; patience, gentle Audrey.

Audrey. Faith, the priest was good enough, for all the old gentleman's saying.

Touchstone. A most wicked Sir Oliver, Audrey, a most vile Martext. But, Audrey, there is a youth here in the forest lays claim to you.

Audrey. Ay, I know who 'tis; he hath no interest in me in the world. Here comes the man you mean.

Touchstone. It is meat and drink to me to see a clown. By my troth, we that have good wits have much to answer for; we shall be flouting; we cannot hold.[1]

Enter WILLIAM.

William. Good even, Audrey.

Audrey. God ye good even,[2] William.

William. And good even to you, sir.

Touchstone. Good even, gentle friend. Cover thy head, cover thy head; nay, prithee, be cover'd. How old are you, friend ?

William. Five and twenty, sir.

Touchstone. A ripe age. Is thy name William ?

William. William, sir.

Touchstone. A fair name. Wast born i' the forest here ?

William. Ay, sir, I thank God.

Touchstone. "Thank God,"—a good answer. Art rich ?

William. Faith, sir, so-so.

---

[1] "We cannot hold," i.e., we cannot restrain ourselves; we must have our gibe.

[2] "God ye good even," i.e., God give you good even.

Touchstone. " So-so " is good, very good, very excellent good ;
—and yet it is not ; it is but so-so.   Art thou wise ?

William. Ay, sir, I have a pretty wit.

Touchstone. Why, thou say'st well.   I do now remember a saying, "The fool doth think he is wise, but the wise man knows
himself to be a fool."   The heathen philosopher, when he had a
desire to eat a grape, would open his lips when he put it into his
mouth ; meaning thereby that grapes were made to eat and lips
to open.   You do love this maid ?

William. I do, sir.

Touchstone. Give me your hand.   Art thou learned ?

William. No, sir.

Touchstone. Then learn this of me : to have is to have ; for it
is a figure in rhetoric that drink, being pour'd out of a cup into a
glass, by filling the one doth empty the other ; for all your writers
do consent that *ipse* is he ; now, you are not *ipse*, for I am he.

William. Which he, sir ?

Touchstone. He, sir, that must marry this woman.   Therefore,
you clown, abandon—which is in the vulgar leave—the society
—which in the boorish is company—of this female—which in
the common is woman ; which together is, abandon the society
of this female, or, clown, thou perishest ; or, to thy better understanding, diest ; or, to wit, I kill thee, make thee away, translate
thy life into death, thy liberty into bondage ; I will deal in poison with thee, or in bastinado,[1] or in steel ; I will bandy[2] with
thee in faction ; I will o'errun thee with policy ; I will kill thee
a hundred and fifty ways ; therefore tremble, and depart.

Audrey. Do, good William.

William. God rest you merry, sir.   [*Exit.*

Enter CORIN.

Corin. Our master and mistress seek you ; come, away, away !

Touchstone. Trip, Audrey ! trip, Audrey ! —I attend, I attend.
                                                    [*Exeunt.*

---

[1] A blow with a cudgel.   [2] Contend.

SCENE II. *The Forest.*

Enter ORLANDO *and* OLIVER.

Orlando. Is't possible that on so little acquaintance you should like her? that but seeing you should love her? and loving woo? and wooing she should grant? and will you persever[1] to enjoy her?

Oliver. Neither call the giddiness of it in question, the poverty of her, the small acquaintance, my sudden wooing, nor her sudden consenting; but say with me, I love Aliena; say with her that she loves me; consent with both that we may enjoy each other. It shall be to your good; for my father's house and all the revenue that was old Sir Rowland's will I estate upon you, and here live and die a shepherd.

Orlando. You have my consent. Let your wedding be to-morrow. Thither will I invite the Duke and all's contented followers. Go you and prepare Aliena; for look you, here comes my Rosalind.

Enter ROSALIND.

Rosalind. God save you, brother.

Oliver. And you, fair sister.   [*Exit.*

Rosalind. O my dear Orlando, how it grieves me to see thee wear thy heart in a scarf!

Orlando. It is my arm.

Rosalind. I thought thy heart had been wounded with the claws of a lion.

Orlando. Wounded it is, but with the eyes of a lady.

Rosalind. Did your brother tell you how I counterfeited to swoon when he show'd me your handkercher?

Orlando. Ay, and greater wonders than that.

Rosalind. O, I know where you are.[2]— Nay, 'tis true; there was never anything so sudden but the fight of two rams, and Cæsar's

---

[1] Persevere (accent on the second syllable).
[2] " Where you are," i.e., what you mean.

thrasonical [1] brag of " I came, saw, and overcame." [2]   For your brother and my sister no sooner met but they look'd, no sooner look'd but they lov'd, no sooner lov'd but they sigh'd, no sooner sigh'd but they ask'd one another the reason, no sooner knew the reason but they sought the remedy; and in these degrees have they made a pair of stairs to marriage which they will climb incontinent; [3] they are in the very wrath of love, and they will together; clubs cannot part them.

Orlando. They shall be married to-morrow, and I will bid the Duke to the nuptial. But, O, how bitter a thing it is to look into happiness through another man's eyes !   By so much the more shall I to-morrow be at the height of heart-heaviness, by how much I shall think my brother happy in having what he wishes for.

Rosalind. Why, then, to-morrow I cannot serve your turn for Rosalind ?

Orlando. I can live no longer by thinking.

Rosalind. I will weary you then no longer with idle talking. Know of me then—for now I speak to some purpose—that I know you are a gentleman of good conceit.[4]   I speak not this that you should bear a good opinion of my knowledge, insomuch I say I know you are; neither do I labor for a greater esteem than may in some little measure draw a belief from you, to do yourself good and not to grace me.   Believe then, if you please, that I can do strange things.   I have, since I was three year old, convers'd with a magician, most profound in his art and yet not damnable.[5]   If you do love Rosalind so near the heart as your gesture [6] cries it out, when your brother marries Aliena, shall you marry her.   I know into what straits of fortune she is driven; and

---

[1] Extravagantly boastful.

[2] It was after his swift and total defeat of Pharnaces, King of Pontus, at Zela (45 B.C.), that Julius Cæsar sent to the Roman senate the celebrated dispatch, *Veni, vidi, vici* (" I came, I saw, I overcame ").

[3] Immediately.   [4] Intelligence.

[5] Worthy of condemnation.   [6] Speech and action.

it is not impossible to me, if it appear not inconvenient to you, to set her before your eyes to-morrow, human as she is and without any danger.

Orlando. Speak'st thou in sober meanings?

Rosalind. By my life, I do; which I tender dearly,[1] though I say I am a magician.[2] Therefore put you in your best array; bid your friends; for if you will be married to-morrow, you shall, and to Rosalind, if you will.

Enter Silvius *and* Phebe.

Look, here comes a lover of mine and a lover of hers.

Phebe. Youth, you have done me much ungentleness,
To show the letter that I writ[3] to you.

Rosalind. I care not if I have; it is my study
To seem despiteful and ungentle to you.
You are there followed by a faithful shepherd;
Look upon him, love him; he worships you.

Phebe. Good shepherd, tell this youth what 'tis to love.

Silvius. It is to be all made of sighs and tears;
And so am I for Phebe.

Phebe. And I for Ganymede.

Orlando. And I for Rosalind.

Rosalind. And I for no woman.

Silvius. It is to be all made of faith and service;
And so am I for Phebe.

Phebe. And I for Ganymede.

Orlando. And I for Rosalind.

Rosalind. And I for no woman.

Silvius. It is to be all made of fantasy,
All made of passion and all made of wishes,

---

[1] "Tender dearly," i.e., value highly.

[2] Under the provisions of statutes in force in England in Shakespeare's time, the practice of witchcraft, magic, etc., was an offense punishable with one year's imprisonment for the first conviction, and death and forfeiture of goods for the second.   [3] Old form of "wrote."

All adoration, duty, and observance,[1]
All humbleness, all patience and impatience,
All purity, all trial, all observance;
And so am I for Phebe.

Phebe. And so am I for Ganymede.

Orlando. And so am I for Rosalind.

Rosalind. And so am I for no woman.

Phebe. If this be so, why blame you me to love you?

Silvius. If this be so, why blame you me to love you?

Orlando. If this be so, why blame you me to love you?

Rosalind. Who do you speak to, "Why blame you me to love you?"

Orlando. To her that is not here, nor doth not hear.

Rosalind. Pray you, no more of this; 'tis like the howling of Irish wolves[2] against the moon.—[*To Silvius*] I will help you, if I can.—[*To Phebe*] I would love you, if I could.—To-morrow meet me all together.—[*To Phebe*] I will marry you, if ever I marry woman, and I'll be married to-morrow.—[*To Orlando*] I will satisfy you, if ever I satisfi'd man, and you shall be married to-morrow.—[*To Silvius*] I will content you, if what pleases you contents you, and you shall be married to-morrow.—[*To Orlando*] As you love Rosalind, meet.—[*To Silvius*] As you love Phebe, meet;—and as I love no woman, I'll meet.—So fare you well; I have left you commands.

Silvius. I'll not fail, if I live.

Phebe. Nor I.

Orlando. Nor I.   [*Exeunt.*

SCENE III. *The Forest.*

Enter TOUCHSTONE *and* AUDREY.

Touchstone. To-morrow is the joyful day, Audrey; to-morrow will we be married.

---

[1] Readiness to serve.

[2] The howling of a pack of wolves is monotonous and dismal whenever and wherever heard.

Audrey. I do desire it with all my heart; and I hope it is no dishonest desire to desire to be a woman of the world.[1] Here come two of the banish'd Duke's pages.

Enter two Pages.

First Page. Well met, honest gentleman.

Touchstone. By my troth, well met. Come, sit, sit, and a song.

Second Page. We are for you; sit i' the middle.

First Page. Shall we clap into't roundly, without hawking or spitting or saying we are hoarse, which are the only[2] prologues to a bad voice?

Second Page. I' faith, i' faith; and both in a tune, like two gypsies on a horse.

SONG.

It was a lover and his lass,
  With a hey, and a ho, and a hey nonino,
That o'er the green cornfield did pass
  In the springtime, the only pretty ringtime,
When birds do sing, hey ding a ding, ding;
Sweet lovers love the spring.

Between the acres of the rye,
  With a hey, and a ho, and a hey nonino,
These pretty country folks would lie,
  In springtime, etc.

This carol they began that hour,
  With a hey, and a ho, and a hey nonino,
How that a life was but a flower
  In springtime, etc.

And therefore take the present time,
  With a hey, and a ho, and a hey nonino;
For love is crowned with the prime
  In springtime, etc.

---

[1] " A woman of the world," i.e., a married woman.
[2] " The only," i.e., only the.

Touchstone. Truly, young gentlemen, though there was no great matter in the ditty, yet the note was very untunable.

First Page. You are deceiv'd, sir; we kept time, we lost not our time.

Touchstone. By my troth, yes; I count it but time lost to hear such a foolish song. God be wi' you; and God mend your voices!—Come, Audrey.   [*Exeunt.*

SCENE IV. *The Forest.*

Enter DUKE Senior, AMIENS, JAQUES, ORLANDO, OLIVER, *and* CELIA.

Duke S. Dost thou believe, Orlando, that the boy
Can do all this that he hath promised?

Orlando. I sometimes do believe, and sometimes do not;
As those that fear they hope, and know they fear.

Enter ROSALIND, SILVIUS, *and* PHEBE.

Rosalind. Patience once more, whiles our compact' is urg'd.—
You say, if I bring in your Rosalind,
You will bestow her on Orlando here?

Duke S. That would I, had I kingdoms to give with her.

Rosalind. And you say you will have her, when I bring her?

Orlando. That would I, were I of all kingdoms king.

Rosalind. You say you'll marry me, if I be willing?

Phebe. That will I, should I die the hour after.

Rosalind. But if you do refuse to marry me,
You'll give yourself to this most faithful shepherd?

Phebe. So is the bargain.

Rosalind. You say that you'll have Phebe, if she will?

Silvius. Though to have her and death were both one thing.

Rosalind. I have promis'd to make all this matter even.—
Keep you your word, O Duke, to give your daughter.—
You yours, Orlando, to receive his daughter.—
Keep your word, Phebe, that you'll marry me,
Or else refusing me, to wed this shepherd.—

Keep your word, Silvius, that you'll marry her,
If she refuse me:—and from hence I go,
To make these doubts all even.　　　*[Exeunt Rosalind and Celia.*
　　Duke S. I do remember in this shepherd boy
Some lively touches of my daughter's favor.
　　Orlando. My lord, the first time that I ever saw him
Methought he was a brother to your daughter;
But, my good lord, this boy is forest-born,
And hath been tutor'd in the rudiments
Of many desperate [1] studies by his uncle,
Whom he reports to be a great magician,
Obscured in the circle of this forest.

Enter TOUCHSTONE *and* AUDREY.

　　Jaques. There is, sure, another flood toward,[2] and these couples
are coming to the ark.　Here comes a pair of very strange beasts,
which in all tongues are called fools.
　　Touchstone. Salutation and greeting to you all !
　　Jaques. Good my lord, bid him welcome.　This is the motley-
minded gentleman that I have so often met in the forest; he
hath been a courtier, he swears.
　　Touchstone. If any man doubt that, let him put me to my
purgation.　I have trod a measure;[3] I have flatter'd a lady;
I have been politic with my friend, smooth with mine enemy:
I have undone three tailors; I have had four quarrels, and like
to have fought one.
　　Jaques. And how was that ta'en up ?[4]
　　Touchstone. Faith, we met, and found the quarrel was upon
the seventh cause.
　　Jaques. How seventh cause ?—Good my lord, like this fellow.
　　Duke S. I like him very well.
　　Touchstone. God 'ild you, sir; I desire you of the like.　I press
in here, sir, amongst the rest of the country copulatives,[5] to swear

---

[1] Unlawful.　　　　[2] At hand.　　　　[3] Stately dance.
[4] Taken up, i.e., made up.　　　　[5] Candidates for marriage.

and to forswear; according as marriage binds and blood breaks. A poor virgin, sir, an ill-favor'd thing, sir, but mine own; a poor humor of mine, sir, to take that that no man else will. Rich honesty dwells like a miser, sir, in a poor house; as your pearl in your foul oyster.

Duke S. By my faith, he is very swift and sententious.[1]

Touchstone. According to the fool's bolt,[2] sir, and such dulcet diseases.

Jaques. But, for the seventh cause; how did you find the quarrel on the seventh cause?

Touchstone. Upon a lie seven times removed,—bear your body more seeming,[3] Audrey,—as thus, sir. I did dislike the cut of a certain courtier's beard; he sent me word, if I said his beard was not cut well, he was in the mind it was; this is call'd the Retort Courteous. If I sent him word again it was not well cut, he would send me word he cut it to please himself; this is call'd the Quip [4] Modest. If, again, it was not well cut, he disabled my judgment; this is call'd the Reply Churlish. If again it was not well cut, he would answer, I spake not true; this is call'd the Reproof Valiant. If again it was not well cut, he would say, I lied; this is call'd the Countercheck Quarrelsome; and so to the Lie Circumstantial and the Lie Direct.

Jaques. And how oft did you say his beard was not well cut?

Touchstone. I durst go no further than the Lie Circumstantial, nor he durst not give me the Lie Direct; and so we measur'd swords and parted.

Jaques. Can you nominate in order now the degrees of the lie?

Touchstone. O sir, we quarrel in print, by the book, as you have books for good manners. I will name you the degrees. The first, the Retort Courteous; the second, the Quip Modest; the third, the Reply Churlish; the fourth, the Reproof Valiant; the fifth, the Countercheck Quarrelsome; the sixth, the Lie with

---

[1] " Swift and sententious," i.e., ready-witted.
[2] " The fool's bolt is soon shot " is proverbial.
[3] Seemly.   [4] A quip is a gibe.

Circumstance; the seventh, the Lie Direct. All these you may avoid but the Lie Direct; and you may avoid that, too, with an If. I knew when seven justices could not take up a quarrel, but when the parties were met themselves, one of them thought but of an If, as, "If you said so, then I said so;" and they shook hands and swore brothers. Your If is the only peace-maker; much virtue in If.

Jaques. Is not this a rare fellow, my lord? He's as good at anything, and yet a fool.

Duke S. He uses his folly like a stalking-horse,[1] and under the presentation of that he shoots his wit.

Enter HYMEN, ROSALIND, *and* CELIA.

[*Still music.*

Hymen. Then is there mirth in heaven,
When earthly things made even
Atone together.[2]
Good Duke, receive thy daughter;
Hymen[3] from heaven brought her,
Yea, brought her hither,
That thou mightst join her hand with his
Whose heart within her bosom is.

Rosalind. [*To Duke*] To you I give myself, for I am yours.—
[*To Orlando*] To you I give myself, for I am yours.

Duke S. If there be truth in sight, you are my daughter.

Orlando. If there be truth in sight, you are my Rosalind

Phebe. If sight and shape be true,
Why, then, my love, adieu!

Rosalind. [*To Duke*] I'll have no father, if you be not he.—
[*To Orlando*] I'll have no husband, if you be not he.—
[*To Phebe*] Nor ne'er wed woman, if you be not she.

---

[1] A stalking-horse is a horse, or the semblance of one, by means of which the sportsman conceals himself from his prey.

[2] "Atone together," i.e., harmonize.   [3] The god of marriage.

Hymen. Peace, ho ! I bar confusion.
'Tis I must make conclusion
 Of these most strange events.
Here's eight that must take hands
To join in Hymen's bands,
 If truth holds true contents'.—
 You and you no cross shall part;—
 You and you are heart in heart;—
 You to his love must accord,
 Or have a woman to your lord;—
You and you are sure together,
As the winter to foul weather.—
Whiles a wedlock hymn we sing,
Feed yourselves with questioning;
That reason wonder may diminish,
How thus we met, and these things finish.

SONG.

 Wedding is great Juno's crown ;
  O blessed bond of board and bed !
 'Tis Hymen peoples every town ;
  High wedlock then be honored.
 Honor, high honor and renown,
 To Hymen, god of every town !

Duke S. O my dear niece, welcome thou art to me !—
Even daughter, welcome, in no less degree.
 Phebe. I will not eat my word, now thou art mine ;
Thy faith my fancy to thee doth combine.[1]

Enter JAQUES DE BOIS.

Jaques de Bois. Let me have audience for a word or two.
I am the second son of old Sir Rowland,
That bring these tidings to this fair assembly.

---

[1] Bind.

Duke Frederick, hearing how that every day
Men of great worth resorted to this forest,
Address'd [1] a mighty power; which were on foot,
In his own conduct, purposely to take
His brother here and put him to the sword;
And to the skirts of this wild wood he came,
Where meeting with an old religious man,
After some question [2] with him, was converted
Both from his enterprise and from the world,
His crown bequeathing to his banish'd brother,
And all their lands restor'd to them again
That were with him exil'd.   This to be true,
I do engage my life.
   Duke S.   Welcome, young man;
Thou offer'st fairly to thy brothers' wedding.
To one his lands withheld, and to the other
A land itself at large, a potent dukedom.
First, in this forest let us do those ends
That here were well begun and well begot;
And after, every of this happy number
That have endur'd shrewd [3] days and nights with us
Shall share the good of our returned fortune,
According to the measure of their states.
Meantime, forget this new-fall'n dignity,
And fall into our rustic revelry. —
Play, music! — And you, brides and bridegrooms all,
With measure heap'd in joy, to the measures fall.
   Jaques. Sir, by your patience. — If I heard you rightly,
The Duke hath put on a religious life
And thrown into neglect the pompous court?
   Jaques de Bois. He hath.
   Jaques. To him will I; out of these convertites [4]
There is much matter to be heard and learn'd. —
[*To Duke*] You to your former honor I bequeath;

---

   [1] Made ready.   [2] Discourse.   [3] Evil.   [4] Converts.

Your patience and your virtue well deserves it. —
[*To Orlando*] You to a love that your true faith doth merit. —
[*To Oliver*] You to your land and love and great allies. —
[*To Silvius*] You to a long and well-deserved bed. —
[*To Touchstone*] And you to wrangling; for thy loving voyage
Is but for two months victual'd. — So, to your pleasures;
I am for other than for dancing measures.

   Duke S. Stay, Jaques, stay.

   Jaques. To see no pastime I; what you would have I'll stay
to know at your abandon'd cave.   [*Exit.*

   Duke S. Proceed, proceed; we will begin these rites,
As we do trust they'll end, in true delights.   [*A dance.*

EPILOGUE.

   Rosalind. It is not the fashion to see the lady the epilogue;
but it is no more unhandsome than to see the lord the prologue.
If it be true that good wine needs no bush,[1] 'tis true that a good
play needs no epilogue; yet to good wine they do use good
bushes, and good plays prove the better by the help of good
epilogues. What a case am I in, then, that am neither a good
epilogue nor cannot insinuate with you in the behalf of a good
play! I am not furnish'd[2] like a beggar, therefore to beg will
not become me. My way is to conjure you; and I'll begin with
the women. I charge you, O women, for the love you bear to
men, to like as much of this play as please you; — and I charge
you, O men, for the love you bear to women — as I perceive, by
your simpering, none of you hates them — that between you and
the women the play may please. If I were a woman[3] I would

---

   1 " Good wine," etc. " It appears formerly to have been the custom to
hang a tuft of ivy at the door of a vintner. I suppose ivy was chosen rather
than any other plant as it has relation to Bacchus." (Steevens's note, quoted
by Furness.)

   2 Dressed.

   3 There were no actresses on the stage in England before the time of

kiss as many of you as had beards that pleased me, complexions that lik'd me,[1] and breaths that I defied not;[2] and, I am sure, as many as have good beards or good faces or sweet breaths will, for my kind offer, when I make curtsy, bid me farewell.

[*Exeunt.*

Charles II. Women's parts in plays were performed by men. Samuel Pepys has this note in his Diary: "January 3, 1660.—To the theater, where was acted The Beggar's Bush, it being very well done; and here, the first time that ever I saw a woman come upon the stage."

[1] " That lik'd me," i.e., that I liked.

[2] " That I defied not," i.e., that were not repulsive to me.

www.ingramcontent.com/pod-product-compliance
Lightning Source LLC
Chambersburg PA
CBHW020809020726
47495CB00008B/2649